First published in the
United Kingdom in 2016 by
Portico
1 Gower Street
London
WC1E 6HD

An imprint of Pavilion Books Company Ltd

ISBN 978-1-91023-225-5

A CIP catalogue record for this book is available
from the British Library.

10 9 8 7 6 5 4 3 2 1

Reproduction by Mission Productions Ltd, Hong Kong
Printed and bound by Times Offset (M) Sdn Bhd,
Malaysia

This book can be ordered direct from the
publisher at www.pavilionbooks.com

CooL Nature

FiLLed with facts & projects FOR KiDs OF ALL Ages

AMY-JANE BEER

PAVILION

Contents

Welcome to *Cool Nature*

Hello. Fancy you being here. Right here, looking at this page. It's amazing, isn't it? Not so much that you're reading this book, perhaps (after all, it is cool), but the fact that you're here at all. You, your family, your friends and acquaintances, your pets – not to mention the billions of other organisms we share the planet with. We are all the result of an extraordinary sequence of events, coincidences and serendipities. Colliding space debris, planetary orbits, the random chemical miracle of life, the deadly lottery of genetic mutation and natural selection, and the unbelievably unlikely success of every one of your direct ancestors in producing another generation. It has all led to you being here with eyes sharp enough to detect the tiny differences in electromagnetic radiation being reflected off the pigment in this page, and a brain that resolves that image into words and links them to concepts, which form pictures in your mind so that I can make you think of plant sex organs just by typing F-L-O-W-E-R. See? And while I'm on the subject, how cool are flowers? Organs designed purely for the purposes of convincing other sentient organisms to act as go-betweens delivering packets of genetic material from one partner to another. Nature is exceptionally cool.

I'm a biologist, so my expertise centres on living things – but actually the standard territories of science are rather meaningless. Indeed, it's often the intersections and overlaps among disciplines and the no-man's-land in between that sprout the most original and exciting developments, so yes, give me chemistry, give me geology too, and I'd love some physics, a dash of astronomy and even … oh, go on, then, let's have some maths. Nature is in it all and all of it is Nature, and none of it requires us in order to be. Which makes for a pretty exciting place to start a book.

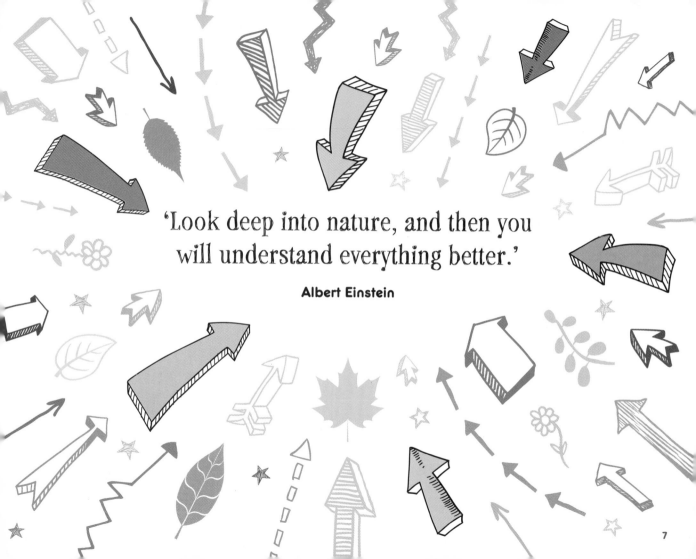

'Look deep into nature, and then you will understand everything better.'

Albert Einstein

Timeline

4.6 billion years BC The Earth forms

3.5 billion years BC Simple living organisms arise

3 billion years BC Early plants begin photosynthesising – and releasing oxygen into the atmosphere

1 billion years BC Complex mutlicellular life evolves

600 million years BC The first animals

472 million years BC Land plants

360 million years BC The first amphibians

240 million years BC The first mammals

200–65 million years BC The age of dinosaurs

180 million years BC The supercontinent Pangea begins to break up

2.4 million years BC Early humans begin manufacturing stone tools in Africa

250,000 BC Anatomically modern humans appear

20,000 BC Humans invent and begin using powered weapons, such as spear throwers and harpoons, to hunt

10,000 BC The dog is domesticated

10,000 BC Last Ice Age ends

9,000 BC Sheep and goats are domesticated

8,000 BC Crops, such as potatoes, beans and rice begin to be cultivated

7,000 BC Wheat, flax and corn begin to be cultivated

c350 BC The Greek philosopher Aristole begins a biological classification of 500 species of animal

c300 BC Aristotle's student Theophrastus begins studying and classifying plants

c50 BC Pliny the Elder writes a 37-volume *Naturalis Historia*, summarising current knowledge of zoology, geography and astronomy

1543 AD Nicolas Copernicus publishes his heliocentric theory (that the Sun, not the Earth is the centre of the solar system)

1627 The wild ancestor of domestic cattle, the aurochs, goes extinct

1665 Robert Hooke describes cells for the first time

1667 John Ray divides flowering plants into monocots and dicots

1673 Antonie van Leeuwenhoek shows the results of his new invention – the microscope

1677 Antonie van Leeuwenhoek discovers protists

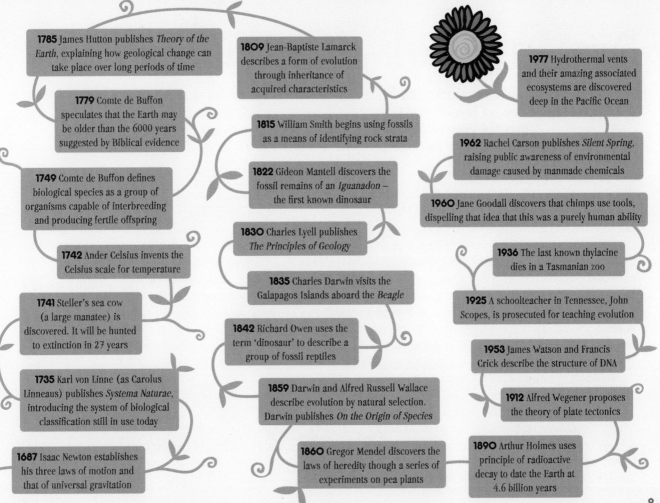

1785 James Hutton publishes *Theory of the Earth*, explaining how geological change can take place over long periods of time

1779 Comte de Buffon speculates that the Earth may be older than the 6000 years suggested by Biblical evidence

1749 Comte de Buffon defines biological species as a group of organisms capable of interbreeding and producing fertile offspring

1742 Ander Celsius invents the Celsius scale for temperature

1741 Steller's sea cow (a large manatee) is discovered. It will be hunted to extinction in 27 years

1735 Karl von Linne (as Carolus Linneaus) publishes *Systema Naturae*, introducing the system of biological classification still in use today

1687 Isaac Newton establishes his three laws of motion and that of universal gravitation

1809 Jean-Baptiste Lamarck describes a form of evolution through inheritance of acquired characteristics

1815 William Smith begins using fossils as a means of identifying rock strata

1822 Gideon Mantell discovers the fossil remains of an *Iguanadon* – the first known dinosaur

1830 Charles Lyell publishes *The Principles of Geology*

1835 Charles Darwin visits the Galapagos Islands aboard the *Beagle*

1842 Richard Owen uses the term 'dinosaur' to describe a group of fossil reptiles

1859 Darwin and Alfred Russell Wallace describe evolution by natural selection. Darwin publishes *On the Origin of Species*

1860 Gregor Mendel discovers the laws of heredity though a series of experiments on pea plants

1977 Hydrothermal vents and their amazing associated ecosystems are discovered deep in the Pacific Ocean

1962 Rachel Carson publishes *Silent Spring*, raising public awareness of environmental damage caused by manmade chemicals

1960 Jane Goodall discovers that chimps use tools, dispelling that idea that this was a purely human ability

1936 The last known thylacine dies in a Tasmanian zoo

1925 A schoolteacher in Tennessee, John Scopes, is prosecuted for teaching evolution

1953 James Watson and Francis Crick describe the structure of DNA

1912 Alfred Wegener proposes the theory of plate tectonics

1890 Arthur Holmes uses principle of radioactive decay to date the Earth at 4.6 billion years

The Earth inside out

Dear old Earth is the third planet in our solar system and the only one we know that is capable of supporting life. But life occupies only the thinnest layer of the Earth's bulk – sometimes compared to the bloom on a plum skin. What about the rest?

The low-down

Did you ever think about digging a hole to Australia? OK, it's impossible – 12,700km through molten rock and super-heated radioactive metal. You know that now. But have you wondered how far we've actually got? Even with our mightiest mining technology, the deepest we've managed to burrow so far is an underwhelming 12km. That's less than 0.1 per cent of the way – barely a pinprick in the Earth's skin.

Journey to the centre of the Earth

Fortunately, given that no one has or ever will be even remotely close to the centre of the Earth, there are other ways to discover what it's made of. That there's a massive quantity of iron is apparent from the fact that Earth acts as a gigantic magnet. Lucky for us that it does, as the magnetic field deflects the solar wind – an unending stream of charged particles pouring out of the Sun.

The depths of the layers inside the Earth have been calculated from the way seismic waves from earthquakes are reflected and refracted – much as the properties of other solid materials can be inferred from the way they bounce or deflect waves of light or X-rays.

The structure of the Earth has been compared to a Scotch egg, with a thin outer coat of breadcrumbs (the crust), thick layers of sausage meat (mantle) and egg white (outer core), and a central yolk (inner core).

That's one hell of a Scotch egg!

The **inner core** is made of iron and nickel, so dense that one cubic metre weighs about 13 tonnes – about four times heavier than rock. It may take the form of either a crystalline solid or a plasma with solid-like properties – either way it is super-heated to about 5,500°C.

The **outer core** has the same metal composition as the inner core, but in a liquid molten state.

Finally the **crust**, which is only 60km thick at most, is actually more like a thin eggshell. This fragile outer layer is continually cracking and healing.

The **mantle** is the thickest layer and is solid but ductile rock, which can flow very slowly over time, like ice. Small pockets of molten rock, or magma, work their way up through the mantle, expanding like bubbles in a soft drink, sometimes welling up through cracks in the crust as lava.

Earth is the only planet we know of with plate tectonics (see p. 24).

Geology rocks!

Geologists divide rocks into three classes, depending on the way they form. Finer distinctions are based on differences in looks, texture and chemical composition.

Igneous rocks

Form when molten rock (magma) is allowed to cool. This cooling can happen quickly, as when the magma emerges as lava through openings in the Earth's crust, or slowly deep beneath the surface. Very rapidly cooled lava becomes glassy. Bubbles of gas are sometimes trapped inside igneous rocks as they cool, resulting in something that looks like a holey Swiss cheese.

Basalt is an igneous rock that lies under almost all the world's oceans, making it the Earth's most abundant rock. It is also found on the Moon and Mars, which show features of ancient volcanism.

Sedimentary rocks

Form by gradual accumulation of matter (sediment) on the bottom of a sea or lake bed. These are the rocks in which fossils are found.

Chalk is a sedimentary rock made from the remains of tiny prehistoric organisms, mostly a group of algae known as coccolithophores. In life, each coccolithophore was enclosed in a tiny calcite shell. These shells can still be identified under a powerful microscope in samples of crushed chalk.

Metamorphic rocks

These have been subject to intense heat and pressure, deep in the Earth's crust. Some so-called foliated types have a layered appearance, often with bands or ribbons of colour running through them.

Slate is a metamorphic rock formed when shale (a sedimentary rock) is subject to extreme heat and pressure. Slate retains the layered structure seen in shale – making it easy to split into large, flat pieces ideal for roof tiles or flooring.

The rock cycle

Nothing in Nature lasts forever – including rock. Rock of any type will eventually end up converted into another form – pebbles of metamorphic rock can be eroded into sand, then be incorporated into sedimentary formations, and igneous rock can be pushed down deep into the Earth's crust and converted into metamorphic forms.

Rock spotting

To help you identify rocks, look for clues such as particles, bubbles, fossils, crystals, texture, layers, bands or ribbons of colour or tone. Hardness is important – for example, can you scratch it and leave a mark with your fingernail or a coin?

The columnar basalt making up the Giant's Causeway in Northern Ireland is the result of rapid cooling of an ancient lava flow, and not (sadly) the work of legendary giant Finn McCool. Cooling causes contraction that creates a regular network of vertical cracks. Columns are usually hexagonal, though other shapes are known.

Fascinating fossils

Much of our knowledge of prehistory and evolution has been informed by fossils – the preserved remains of animals and plants that lived anything from 10,000 to 3.5 billion years ago.

Oldies but goodies

The oldest known fossils are microscopic cellular filaments invisible to the naked eye and barely recognisable as life. They are **cyanobacteria**, a wide variety of which still thrive on Earth today – also known as blue-green algae.

Aren't you well preserved?

Usually it's the hard parts of ancient animals and plants, such as bones, teeth, shells and wood, that form fossils. Soft or semi-soft parts are much more likely to decay before they can be preserved, and so are much more rare, but every now and then fossils turn up with staggering preservation of softer tissues such as feathers, skin, internal organs and gut contents.

The best fossilisation is achieved when an ancient organism is quickly and completely engulfed by a fine-textured material such as **silt**. The finer the material, the better the potential preservation.

Mudslides on the prehistoric continent of Laurentia about 454–520 million years ago led to the formation of one of the world's most famous fossils sites, the **Burgess Shale**, in what is now the Canadian Rockies. The formation contains extraordinary fossils of tens of thousands of mainly soft-bodied creatures that have revolutionised our understanding of the variety of prehistoric life.

A sticky situation

On a small scale, even more perfect preservation occurred when tiny animals such as insects were trapped in sticky tree sap, which hardened to form **amber**.

Fossils preserved this way look much the same now as on the day they died, up to 150 million years ago.

Fossil foraging

There are great fossil-hunting sites in all regions of the UK. Consult a guidebook or website to find one near you. Beaches and quarries are often a good option, but check the status of the site first – some are designated Sites of Special Scientific Interest, and are strictly 'no take'. Also remember to check tides and make sure you have permission to enter quarry workings. Consider protective headgear if you're planning to spend time at the base of cliffs.

You don't need special tools – many finds are made just by turning over pieces of rock. If you wish, you can use a small hammer to open rocks along their natural fracture planes, but knowing which to open requires some expertise. There's a code of conduct among fossil hunters that requires you not to spoil things for others – so if you find a large fossil in the rocks, please don't try and hack it out!

Did you know?

Trace fossils are preserved forms that don't actually include parts of the organism itself – for example, the spooky footprints of dinosaurs or ancient humans, preserved nests and burrows, and dung. Fossil poos have their own scientific name – coprolites.

I'm 500 million years old, you know!

Dinosaurs!

As any four-year-old will tell you, there is something indescribably cool about dinosaurs, the reptiles that dominated life on Earth for around 135 million years – that's about 100 times longer than humankind has managed so far.

The dinosaurs include the largest animals ever to have walked on land (although not the largest animal ever to have lived – that honour goes to a modern species, the blue whale). But not all dinosaurs were huge – many were rather small, such as *Compsognathus* and *Lesothosaurus*, which were about the size of a large chicken or small goose.

They were a diverse bunch, with species adapted to many of the lifestyles adopted today by birds and land-dwelling mammals – herbivores, hunters, scavengers and omnivores. Dinosaurs could be either solitary or social, and large or small.

Where did they go?
Most of the dinosaurs were wiped out in a **mass extinction** probably triggered by a meteorite strike about 65 million years ago at the end of the **Cretaceous** period. A few that survived went on to diversify into one of the most successful animal groups alive today, the birds.

The distinctive plates of *Stegosaurus* may have had a role in display and temperature regulation – acting like radiator fins.

The largest currently known dinosaur was *Argentinosaurus huinculensis*, estimated at up to 40m long and 50 tonnes in weight.

Tyrannosaurus rex was a hugely successful uber-predator. Fossil remains are widespread and suggest it was one of the last non-bird dinosaurs to go extinct at the end of the Jurassic period.

Know your non-dinos

There were three groups of large reptiles around at the same time as the dinosaurs that are often misleadingly lumped together with them: the flying **pterosaurs** and the marine **ichthyosaurs** and **plesiosaurs**. In fact all three of them have separate origins distinct from the dinosaur lineage.

Are you smarter than a 100 million-year-old?

So, they were around for ages, but were dinosaurs all that clever? Almost certainly not. The infamous velociraptors of *Jurassic Park* had problem-solving intelligence, but the real *Velociraptor* was little more than knee-high to a man, weighed about the same as a small bag of shopping and was probably not much smarter. It also had feathers. In looks and behaviour, the velociraptors depicted in the movies are more like another species, *Deinonychus*, which weighed up to 75kg and may indeed have hunted in packs. If brain size is an indication of smarts, then the brainiest dinosaur might have been the not dissimilar *Troodon*, whose brain-to-body size ratio was comparable to that of modern birds.

Violent volcanoes

Volcanoes occur where a crack opens up in the Earth's crust, allowing magma (molten rock), ash, hot gases and other materials to be ejected and sometimes causing major devastation.

Volcanic activity is commonly associated with the boundaries where tectonic plates (see p. 24) are colliding or growing apart, but they can also appear mid-plate where magma wells up from deep inside the Earth in so-called mantle plumes.

She's gonna blow!

A volcano is usually classified as active if it has erupted in the last 10,000 years. By this definition there are about 1500 active volcanoes on Earth. Of these, about 500 have erupted recently enough for there to be a written record of the event. Some 40 or 50 are probably erupting properly right now, and another 100 or more are undergoing minor eruptions or unrest.

Eruptions are scored according to the Volcanic Explosivity Index (VEI), based on parameters such as the volume of material expelled, duration, plume height and so on. It's a logarithmic scale, like the Moment Magnitude Scale (see p. 27) so each increment marks a tenfold increase in severity.

Did You Know?

Projectiles thrown up out of a volcano are known as pyroclasts or tephras. A tephra is the term used for a fragment that has come to rest on the ground without being incorporated into new rock formations.

Shield volcano

VOLCANIC EXPLOSIVITY INDEX

VEI 0 Effusive. Occurring constantly.
VEI 1 Gentle. Occurring daily.
VEI 2 Explosive. Occurring weekly.
VEI 3 Catastrophic. Occurring every few months.
VEI 4 Cataclysmic. Annually (on average).
VEI 5 Paroxysmic. A decade or more apart (on average).
VEI 6 Colossal. A century or more apart (on average).
VEI 7 Mega-colossal. A millennium or more apart (on average).
VEI 8 Apocalyptic. 10,000 years or more apart (on average).*

* The last VEI 8 eruption was that of Mount Taupo in New Zealand, 26,500 years ago.

Famous eruptions

Toba, Indonesia, 77,000–69,000 BC; VEI 8. Caused a volcanic winter lasting 10 years, and may explain a 'genetic bottleneck' in human evolution, which suggests the global population was reduced to between 3,000 and 10,000 people.

Vesuvius, Italy, 79 CE; VEI 5. Destroyed the cities of Pompeii and Herculaneum, as documented by Pliny the Younger.

Tambora, Indonesia, 1815; VEI 7. Its enormous eruption column lowered global temperatures and led to the following year being dubbed the 'Year Without a Summer', with catastrophic harvests and epidemic disease.

Krakatoa, Indonesia, 1883; VEI 6. Caused 36,417 directly attributable human deaths due to ash fall or tsunamis, and climatic effects that continued for five years.

St Helens, USA, 1980; VEI 5. Triggered the largest landslips and mudslides ever recorded and spewed ash over 11 states.

Eyjafjallajökull, Iceland 2010; VEI 4. Caused an ash cloud that brought European airspace to a standstill; 100,000 flights were cancelled, affecting 10 million passengers – the most significant disruption of air travel since the Second World War.

Cinder cone

Composite volcano

A volcano in your kitchen

This explosive bit of kitchen science is a domestic crowd-pleaser – the reaction is safe but messy, so cover polished or wooden surfaces and stand by with a mop!

You will need

- A deep tray or large bowl and a towel (for catching the mess)
- One empty plastic milk bottle
- Jug for pouring
- Play dough or plasticine (you can also make convincing-looking mountain dough using three parts flour, one part salt, one part used coffee grounds and one part play sand mixed to form a stiff, squidgy dough with a little water)

For the 'lava'

- 200ml warm water
- Washing-up liquid
- Bicarbonate of soda (note, this is not the same as baking powder, but you'll find it in the baking aisle of your supermarket)
- Food colouring (optional)
- 100ml white vinegar (just use the cheap stuff)

Washing-up liquid   White vinegar   Bicarbonate of soda

Countdown to eruption!

(1) Place the open bottle on the tray and use the dough to model your volcano around it, with the opening as the crater.

(2) Add the warm water to the bottle (the heat will give you a much better reaction), and then add a squirt of washing-up liquid and a tablespoon of soda.

(3) In a separate jug, mix a little food colouring with the vinegar.

④ Tip the whole
jug of vinegar
into your volcano
and admire ...

How does it work?

Basically you're mixing an acid (acetic acid – vinegar) with a base (sodium bicarbonate). These react to form carbonic acid, which rapidly converts into water and carbon dioxide gas, which fizzes and foams as it escapes into the air. The end products are harmless, but vinegar in your eye will sting, so please supervise little ones.

Marvellous mountains

Mountains are places of extremes – once considered desolate and threatening, but now admired for their dramatic beauty and wildlife value or enjoyed as gigantic natural adventure playgrounds.

Mountains are formed by volcanic activity or the gradual collision of tectonic plates, which throws up geological crumple zones. No mountain lasts forever though – over millions of years they are worn down by erosion, becoming smoother, rounder and flatter.

When does a hill become a mountain?
It's all relative. Usually a summit is classed as a mountain if it stands well clear of the surrounding landscape, with a certain amount of descent and ascent between it and its neighbours – but the exact requirements vary from country to country. In the UK peaks over 600m are usually considered mountains, but summits of this sort of size would barely register as foothills in the Himalayas.

Living the high life
Living on mountains is tough, not just because of the cooler temperatures and the lack of food, but also because the air is thinner, with fewer molecules of oxygen (and other gases, mainly nitrogen) per lungful. However, a variety of wild animals and plants have adapted well to these challenges.

ANATOMY OF A MOUNTAIN

Mountain life

- The Himalayan jumping spider, found on the flanks of Mount Everest, is thought to be the highest-living animal, at up to 6,700m.
- Alpine choughs have been known to nest above 6,500m and visit the summit ridges of Everest at 8,000m to scavenge from mountain expeditions.
- Yak graze as high as 6,100m.
- *Polylepis* trees form the world's highest forest at up to 4,500m in the Andes.
- The highest-living plant is probably a tiny moss, found at 6,490m in the Himalayas.

Orographic rainfall As air is forced up over the mountain, it cools, and the water vapour in clouds condenses to form rain.

Rain shadow When the air has passed the summit, most of its moisture has been lost, and the area beyond receives much less rain.

Nival zone With year-round lying snow.

Snow line

Alpine zone Resembles Arctic tundra, with small, low-growing, hardy flowering plants, mosses and lichens.

Tree line No trees above this point.

Subalpine zone Home to stunted or dwarf trees, known as *Krummholz*.

Montane zone Typically cloaked in forest.

Foothills

23

The Earth on a plate

Looking at a map of the world, recognising the complementary shapes of the continents is relative child's play. But working out how continents might move generated one of the great scientific debates of the 20th century.

Are you getting my drift?

The idea of **continental drift** – that the continents are gradually moving about – has been around since maps first revealed the complementary shapes of west Africa and eastern South America, and was reinforced by geological similarities and matching fossil records on either side of the Atlantic Ocean. But what made the idea so difficult for many geologists to accept was that no one could explain how it was happening. After all, the Earth's crust seems pretty solid and, more than that, the rock underlying the oceans (basalt) is much denser than that which makes up the bulk of the continents (granite).

How it works

The Earth's crust is made up of two layers.
The **lithosphere** is a solid surface layer that effectively floats on a layer of molten rock called the **aesthenosphere**. The lithosphere is not a solid shell, but a jigsaw of plates. Some of these plates are growing along boundaries where molten rock wells up from below. Most of these are hidden under the sea – forming **mid-ocean ridges**.

Crash, bang, wallop

There are also **subduction zones** where one plate slips under another (usually a dense ocean-floor plate under a buoyant continental one) and **collision boundaries** where plates crunch together and throw up mountainous crumple zones. Elsewhere plates jostle and scrape past each other, causing earthquakes.

Hmmm, where does this piece of lithosphere plate go?

Magnets point the way

The most compelling evidence for plate tectonics came in the form of **palaeomagnetism**. Many rocks and other materials contain minerals that align themselves like compass needles along the Earth's magnetic field when the rock is forming. This alignment is permanent, so the rock carries a magnetic clue to its longitude location at the time it was formed. Every now and then, the Earth's magnetic field reverses – north becomes south and vice versa. These reversals are recorded in the rocks and also give an indication of age. The rocks either side of spreading ocean ridges are banded with these magnetic reversals, giving an indication of the speed of continental drift – telling us that the continents either side of the Atlantic Ocean are moving apart at about 25mm a year.

Did you know?

The theory of plate tectonics was first proposed by meteorologist Alfred Wegener in 1912. Other scientists followed Wegener's work with supporting evidence, but it was 50 years before the theory was generally accepted.

Earthquake!

The Earth's surface is rattled by approximately half a million earthquakes ever year – about 100,000 of these are strong enough to be noticed by people, and about 100 are strong enough to cause damage.

Earthquakes occur where sections of the Earth's crust collide or scrape past one another along **fault lines.** Such movements are seldom smooth, but happen in a series of high-energy jolts, the largest of which can have disastrous consequences.

Hold on tight

Earthquakes are classified according to a globally recognised **Moment Magnitude Scale.** This is more or less equivalent to the better known scale invented by the seismologist Charles Richter in 1935. Both measure the energy released by a quake. As a rule, tremors need to be Mag 3 to be noticed by people. The occasional earthquakes felt in the UK are about this level.

CoolTimes

EARTHQUAKE IN UK: WE WILL REBUILD

The Moment Magntiude Scale is logarithmic, so every unit increment on the scale denotes a tenfold increase in energy. So a Magnitude 7 earthquake is ten times as powerful as a Mag 6, and a hundred times greater than a Mag 5, and so on.

Seismograph recording

Woah! What's that?!

Can animals predict earthquakes?

After every major earthquake, there are anecdotal reports of animals behaving strangely in the preceding hours or days: dogs barking, bees leaving their hives, cage birds showing unusual restlessness. It's not impossible that they are picking up some warning signs, but what these might be has been difficult to prove, despite extensive research, so such warnings are given varying levels of credibility. Some scientists insist the reports are likely to be influenced by hindsight and that odd behaviours are only remembered and given significance in the event of a subsequent dramatic incident. Others take them much more seriously – in China whole cities have been evacuated based on animal behaviour. What is clear is that warnings based on animal behaviour are not consistent or reliable.

That's seismic!

Tremors are recorded by **seismographs** – the first of these recorded the up-down vibrations of a sheet of paper scrolling past a pen, which was held steady by a sensitive suspension system. Modern seismographers have much more sensitive devices, which record tremors in all directions. You can watch a live feed of global seismographic data at www.earthquakes.bgs.ac.uk.

In terms of damage, where the earthquake occurs is almost as important as how much energy is released. The energy from quakes that take place deep in the Earth's crust, or in the mantle, tends to be dispersed by the time it reaches the surface.

Shallow-focus quakes (those in the upper part of the crust) are more devastating.

Woof woof! Watch out, something's coming!

Desolate deserts

A desert is a landscape receiving little or no rainfall, where life adopts some ingenious adaptations to extremes of temperature and dryness.

Wot, no rain?

Deserts can be hot, such as the Sahara, the Mojave or the Great Sandy Desert of Australia, or cold, like Antarctica, large areas of which go for years between falls of snow. The driest non-polar desert is the Atacama, in Chile, where some weather stations have never recorded rain.

In most deserts, the only reliable source of water is from under the ground, where aquifers feed occasional springs, leading to the formation of oases.

Some like it hot

Away from any water, desert plants and animals must make the most of what little rain falls. Adaptations include restricting activities such as blooming or foraging to the cool hours of the night, collecting dew and storing water. Species can have rapid and opportunistic life cycles: plants can germinate, mature and flower within weeks of rain falling, then produce seeds that can lie dormant for years.

Some animals, such as the Australian water-holding frog, will lie dormant underground until roused by moisture percolating down from above.

Did you know?

Dromedaries (the one-humped Arabian camels) allow their body temperature to sink at night so that it takes them longer to become hot enough to sweat the next day. They also have double rows of eyelashes to keep out dust, soft, wide feet to spread their weight on sand, and grooves under the nostrils to channel any trickling moisture directly back into the mouth.

Extreme living

Deserts are usually sandy or stony because the extremes of temperature and exposure to the elements cause extreme **weathering** of rocks, which shatter and erode. Soils are either absent or very poor, with little organic content, so desert plants must cope not only with lack of water, but also with few opportunities for roots to spread or absorb nutrients.

Eggs-treme heat

In Death Valley, USA, where at Furnace Creek on 10 July 1913 the atmospheric temperature reached a record 57°C (134°F), the rocks are frequently hot enough to cook eggs, although the National Park authorities have recently asked visitors to stop doing so in an attempt to reduce the amount of egg mess accumulating on roadsides and pavements.

29

Secrets of soil

Ancient civilisations understood the value of soil – so much so that in almost every language, our planet is named for it. Yet soil is arguably the most underappreciated and abused of Earth's resources. If you think of soil as just dirt, it's time to think again.

The fundamental value of soil ranks up there with sunlight, oxygen and water. US President Franklin D. Roosevelt was right when he said,

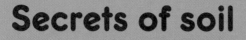

'The nation that destroys its soil destroys itself.'

He was speaking from the experience of the Dust Bowl of the 1930s, an environmental catastrophe resulting from attempts to convert vast areas of prairie to arable farmland. Once ploughed, the fragile soils quickly dried and blew away in dust storms known as 'black blizzards'. An estimated 3.5 million people were displaced.

So, what is soil?

Well, it's complicated – so complicated, in fact, that chemists still don't really have an answer, as each and every soil can have a unique composition. Most include a significant mineral component comprising particles of rock which are graded according to size as:

clay (less than 0.002mm), **silt** (0.002–0.06 mm) and **sand** (0.06–2mm)

Can you see what's down there?

There will also be stones of various sizes, from grit to boulders. A proportion of the mineral particles of any soil may originate from the local bedrock – but lots of it might come from elsewhere – transported by water, ice, wind or by human or animal activity. Each contributing rock type will have a differing chemistry. Then there is the **organic fraction** – the **humus**, which comprises the decayed remains of living plants and animals. Humus gives soil its dark colour, its stickiness, its dirtiness, and much of its nutrient content. It is the glue that binds the particles into *peds* – the crumb-, clod- or prism-like units of soil structure.

The worm that turned

Soils also provide habitats in their own right – for surface dwellers to burrow into and for others to live in. Charles Darwin was a particular fan of earthworms, and rightly so, since their ceaseless activity plays a major role in decomposition and soil conditioning. An average handful of topsoil is also home to many thousands of tiny nematode worms, which feast at a phenomenal rate on billions of bacteria.

Did you know?

Soils provide the basis for terrestrial ecology and agriculture. They also filter and store water and prevent flooding, and they absorb, detoxify and recycle all kinds of organic waste. The Earth's soils store an estimated 15 billion tonnes of carbon – roughly three times more than all the land plants on the planet, thus providing a precious buffer against the greenhouse effect and accelerated climate change.

Creating compost

Nature is a master of recycling. Compost is the best, most natural of fertilisers, and an almost miraculous way of reducing the amount of waste you throw away and enriching your soil at the same time.

You will need
- Organic material that you'd otherwise throw away
- A bit of patience

The key to successful composting is to ensure a roughly equal mix of fresh, wet material – green leaves, veg peelings and so on – and dry fibrous matter such as dead leaves and shredded cardboard.

1 Chop up large items to speed their decay. Large heaps can also take grass clippings, but they shouldn't dominate the mix. Citrus peel is OK in small quantities, but heaps of orange peel will acidify the compost – and be very slow to decay. Be wary of whole live weeds or weed seedheads unless you've already deactivated them by soaking in a bucket of water in the dark for several weeks.

2 Turn the compost every now and then, and if it seems dry, water it or, even better, wee in it (see right).

3 Open compost heaps become havens for wildlife – the moist warmth generated by decaying material is appreciated by amphibians and reptiles, while looser piles of leaves and garden waste are often used by nesting hedgehogs.

Earthworms are a bonus – it's worth adding a few every now and then to help the processes of mixing and decay.

Wiggly wonders
A wormery is a sealed composting unit in which a workforce of worms (usually tiger or brandling worms) speed the process of decay. In addition to raw plant material, wormeries can also take cooked food, including meat. Make sure you add cooked food straight away and seal the lid so flies don't have a chance to lay eggs. The

Let me help!

Wee on your compost – the ammonia in urine is a great nutrient and you'll be saving water used in flushing the loo

Did you know?
★
Stinging nettles have their place in nature but sometimes grow in unwelcome places. If you have to clear a nettle patch, put the clipped stems in a bucket or bin, weight them down with a rock, cover with water, add a lid and leave for two to three weeks. The resulting liquid is a stupendous concentrated plant feed. You can do the same with fleshier plants, such as comfrey, using little or no water.

Humanure

Given time, there's not much that can't be composted. Composting toilets collect solid waste (yes, that does mean poo), with a sprinkling of sawdust for each deposit. The poo rots down over a period of one to two years into amazingly non-stinky compost. Heat generated during the decomposition process is sufficient to kill any dangerous micro-organisms, so the product is safe to use on farms and in gardens. Maybe that's where John Innes 'Number Two' got its name!

liquid that collects in the bottom of the worm bin is a potent fertiliser – you'll need to dilute it with water before putting on the garden.

Angler fish

Planet ocean

An atlas will tell you that ours is a blue planet, two-thirds covered in water, and that these salty oceans are the cradle of life. But how and when did the seas begin, and why are they so crucial to life on Earth?

How it all began

The Earth formed 4.6 billion years ago, coalescing from a whirl of mineral debris and gases swirling around the Sun. For the first few hundred million years, it was a molten mass on which a crust began to form – like the skin on custard. Occasionally the custard was struck by icy comets, which vaporised, creating an atmosphere thick with steam. As the atmosphere cooled, the steam condensed into rain. And the rain never stopped. By 3.8 billion years ago the lowest-lying areas of the globe had filled with water – Earth had its oceans, and the water cycle was established (see p. 38).

The soup of life

Water is an exceptional solvent, and Earth's new seas collected a soup of dissolved molecules, including mineral salts from newly formed rocks and all the essential chemical ingredients for life. Even now, all the chemical reactions required for life to exist need water.

Alternative energy

Instead of sunlight, the communities clustered around hydrothermal vents are reliant on energy released by the oxidation of hydrogen sulphide in a process known as **chemosynthesis**, which was unimagined by biologists only 50 years ago. And yet the high concentrations of ammonia and methane in the vicinity of these vents suggest to some scientists that these may have been the original source of life's basic ingredients.

The big blue

Approximately 5 per cent of the oceans are sunlit by day, and this blue surface zone teems with life, especially in areas where upwelling currents bring nutrients from below, and where long hours of sunlight maximise energy input. The greatest productivity (by which we mean the reproduction of the tiny planktonic algae that form the basis of the food chain) is achieved in the short, intense summers of the high latitudes, while maximum diversity is in the tropics, where intense competition drives life to seek ever more specialised means of making a living.

Vampire squid

Dragon fish

Did you know?

The other 95 per cent of this vast underwater habitat lies in perpetual darkness and is home to myriad mysterious forms: armoured and fragile, fringed and finned, tentacled and glowing, goggle-eyed and snaggle-toothed, including the ones seen here.

Turning salt water into drinking water

This simple trick saves lives by magicking up drinkable water where there is none. In some parts of the world distilled seawater is the main source of potable water for whole communities, but you can try it on a small scale in your back garden or on a windowsill.

Desalination is the process of removing salt and other minerals from water, usually seawater. Over 300 million people worldwide rely on it for their drinking water, especially in areas where rainfall and groundwater are limited, such as the Middle East. Desalination on an industrial scale is expensive and uses a huge amount of energy, but a small-scale **solar still** can do the job using just sunshine. It's a technique widely used by survivalists, sailors and the military.

You will need

- A large, deep bowl, like a washing-up bowl
- A small container made of something heavy, like a glass tumbler or short jar
- A sheet of cling film
- A small, heavy object like a pebble or a ball bearing
- 1 litre of seawater (or use tap water mixed with a spoonful of table salt)

① Put your salt water in the large bowl, then stand the small container in the middle – the water level should be well below the lip.

② Place the cling film over the large bowl and seal the edges carefully, but leaving it loose enough that you can depress the middle slightly.

3 Place the small weight onto the cling film directly over the small inner container so that it makes a slight depression, then leave the whole contraption in a sunny spot.

What happens next?

The water will begin to evaporate, and the resulting vapour, which is pure H_2O, will **condense** on the inside of the plastic, run down to the low point and drip into your container. The salt molecules are left behind in the original liquid, which will become more concentrated and eventually dry up to a salty crust.

If you're feeling more ambitious you could use a large plastic sheet over much larger containers, or dig a pit in a damp area and use that in place of the bowl to extract clean water from the ground.

The water cycle

The water on planet Earth is old. Very, very old. In fact, most of the water in your bath, in your coffee, lapping the beach on your holiday, as well as that transiently present in your body, has been around for billions of years, cycling through a variety of physical states and locations.

The water cycle is driven by energy from the Sun. Heat from the Sun **evaporates** water from rivers, lakes, oceans and damp surfaces, and **sublimates** it from icecaps, glaciers and snow. Water vapour gathers in the atmosphere as clouds, within which individual molecules of water condense into droplets – this happens because each molecule has a positive and a negative end, and the opposite ends of adjacent molecules attract one another.

Is it raining again?

When condensed droplets of water reach a certain size, gravity pulls them downwards as **precipitation** (that's rain, snow or hail, depending on temperatures close to ground level). Gravity acts on liquid water, drawing it downhill in rivers or underground. Some empties directly into the oceans, but a lot will be waylaid in a huge variety of ways – for example as ice, as ground water or tied up in biological systems such as plants or animal bodies.

Alien water

The topography of Mars suggests that rivers once ran there and this is one reason for thinking the red planet may once have supported life. But the temperatures and low atmospheric pressures on Mars today mean that virtually all the water there now exists as ice at the poles or underground, or as atmospheric vapour.

Water shortage?

The vast majority of water on Earth – about 97.4 per cent – is salty, and most of it is in the oceans. Of the 2.6 per cent that is fresh, over two-thirds is bound up in glaciers and most of the rest is underground. In fact, the proportion of Earth's water that is fresh, liquid and available on or near the

THE WATER CYCLE

surface to living things, including humans, is about 0.008 per cent of the total. Not a lot really. So when we talk about saving water, what we actually mean is conserving *fresh* water in a place where it is useful to us, rather than letting it trickle off somewhere less accessible.

Rainforests

A fully formed rainforest is what you get if tropical or temperate landscapes receiving between 2 and 10m of rain every year are left to their own devices for about 4,000 years. Tropical rainforests are widely regarded as the most biodiverse ecosystems on Earth.

Estimates vary, but it's likely that more than half of all the biological species on Earth live in rainforests. Crops such as coffee, banana, sugarcane, yam and mango all originated in tropical rainforests, and thousands of rainforest plants have been identified as potential sources of lifesaving drugs, including more than 2,000 with possible anti-cancer properties.

QUICK FACT

A system resembling a tropical rainforest can regenerate from cleared land in something like a human lifetime, but for the system to regain its full native complexity takes much longer.

Emergent layer Comprising the very tallest trees, some of them as high as 70m, head and shoulders above their neighbours. Such trees are exposed to the full force of the elements, including blistering sun, torrential rain and strong winds, and thus support relatively limited biodiversity. But they make great look-outs for birds of prey and parrots.

Canopy layer The majority of rainforest trees are 30–40m tall and their spreading branches form a more or less continuous layer, creating dense shade below. Most of the forest's biodiversity is associated with this layer, including birds, mammals, invertebrates and a vast array of epiphytic plants, which grow attached to the trunks and branches of the trees. This layer has only begun to be properly explored in the last 40 years. It may contain more than half of all known plant species and a quarter of all insects.

Understorey and shrub layer Smaller trees and bushes, typically with large, spreading leaves that maximise the capture of what little light penetrates the canopy above. The understorey layer is rich in insect life and visited by ground-dwelling animals.

Forest floor This gloomy world receives about 2 per cent of the sunlight that falls on the canopy above and thus supports relatively little plant life. The ground receives a steady rain of leaf litter, seeds and dung from above. When a tree falls, the ground erupts into a dense scramble of plants, all trying to stake a claim to the sunlight that filters through the opening.

'Another continent of life remains to be discovered, not upon the Earth, but one to two hundred feet above it, extending over thousands of square miles.'

WILLIAM BEEBE, NATURALIST, WRITING ABOUT THE RAINFOREST CANOPY IN 1917

Poles apart

The polar regions lie at either end of the Earth's axis, above 60 degrees of latitude. Areas within the polar circles experience midnight sun during summer and 24-hour darkness in winter.

Arctic

The area within the Arctic Circle is mostly ocean, surrounded by land belonging to the polar nations of Canada, Denmark (Greenland and the Faroe Islands), Iceland, Norway, Sweden, Finland, Russia and the United States (Alaska). Historically in winter, the Arctic Ocean froze from shore to shore, but climate change is reducing the area of sea ice and in 2009 commercial shipping was able to begin using the Northwest Passage linking the Atlantic and Pacific oceans for the first time. The reduction in sea ice is posing serious problems for polar bears, which rely on the sea ice for breeding and hunting.

Antarctic

Most of the Antarctic Circle is taken up by the continent of Antarctica, covered for much of the year by ice and snow. Plant life on mainland Antarctica is limited to lichens, mosses and just two species of flowering plant, Antarctic pearlwort and Antarctic hair grass. Terrestrial animals include a single species of insect (a wingless midge), but large numbers of birds, including penguins, skuas, albatrosses and terns, visit the continent to breed.

The sun shines all day – but it's freezing!

The tilt of the Earth means that sunlight reaching the poles strikes the surface obliquely and passes through a thicker layer of atmosphere on its way. So even during summer, when the sun may shine 24 hours a day, the amount of heat energy reaching the surface is much less than at the equator. Furthermore, because much of each polar area is covered in white ice or snow, a large proportion of light that does reach the surface is bounced directly back into space rather than being absorbed. This is known as the **Albedo Effect**.

Midnight sun

The exact duration of the long 'polar day' varies from six months at the poles themselves to 24 hours on the summer solstice at 60 degrees North and South on the Arctic and Antarctic Circles.

Off we go again!

Did you know?

Re-tern ticket

The Arctic tern might be the ultimate polar animal, since it spends its life in one polar circle or the other – or else en route between the two. Adult birds breed in the Arctic, then depart as soon as their chicks are strong enough to make the journey to the Antarctic Circle, 15,000km to the south. As a result, Arctic terns travel more miles in migration and see more hours of daylight per year than any other organism on the planet.

Evolution

Sometimes described as 'Darwin's dangerous idea', the theory of evolution by natural selection is also widely regarded as one of the most perfect scientific theories of all time, having withstood over 150 years of rigorous testing.

What's it all about?
Living things show variation in a wide range of **heritable traits**. Under a given set of circumstances, some of these variants will be more successful than others, and by successful, we mean that on average, individuals with the variant trait *survive and reproduce more successfully* than those without it. Because the trait is genetic, it is passed on to the next generation, and over time, the mechanism leads to specialised forms, which ultimately diverge so much from the ancestral form and other types that they become separate **species**.

Small steps
Darwin recognised that, given enough time, tiny random changes could indeed add up to all the extraordinary diversity of life, despite the fact that the mechanism of genetic inheritance was as yet unknown. Darwin was not the first to suggest evolution. But he was the first person to work out how the change could happen.

Natural selection
This mechanism is **natural selection**. Darwin worked this out after completing a five-year voyage around the world on HMS *Beagle*, but he kept it to himself for 20 years. When another naturalist, Alfred Russell Wallace, wrote to Darwin from the Malay Archipelago outlining the same idea, the two men agreed to publish simultaneous papers on the subject, and Darwin fleshed out the idea in his famous book, *On the Origin of Species*, published in 1859.

My beak's perfect for insect-picking

Mine is great for eating fruits and cacti

My huge beak has evolved for nut and seed crushing

Darwin's finches – specialisation in a nutshell

The birds known as Darwin's finches are a group of about 15 species of drab brown birds found almost exclusively on the Galapagos Islands. The species on different islands vary in the shape of their beaks, from fine insect-picking tweezers to a massive seed-crushing vice, and hint at different lifestyles. As Darwin himself put it, 'Seeing this gradation and diversity of structure in one small, intimately related group of birds, one might really fancy that from an original paucity of birds in this archipelago, one species had been taken and modified for different ends.'

Genetic inheritance

Chances are, you look like your parents. This is no surprise, given that the biological blueprint from which you are assembled contains a 50–50 blend of instructions cribbed directly from the genetic manuals that built your mother and your father.

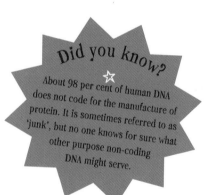

Did you know?

About 98 per cent of human DNA does not code for the manufacture of protein. It is sometimes referred to as 'junk', but no one knows for sure what other purpose non-coding DNA might serve.

It's all in the genes

The concept of the **gene** dates back long before anyone understood how inheritance might actually work. Charles Darwin referred to particles called 'gemmules', which he imagined must blend in the process of fertilisation and carry traits of both parents into a new organism. Unknown to Darwin, even as he published *On the Origin of Species* the rules of inheritance were being discovered by a Moravian monk, Gregor Mendel. Mendel spent years breeding pea plants and recording the way traits such as flower colour, plant height and pod shape were passed from one generation to the next. His work remained little known until 1900 when it was rediscovered and the science of genetics was born.

DNA – the master molecule

By the late 1940s, biologists knew that genetic information was carried on chromosomes – long wiggly structures in the nucleus of biological cells – and that chromosomes were mostly made up of a molecule called **deoxyribonucleic acid**, or **DNA**. The structure of DNA was worked out in Cambridge by James Watson and Francis Crick, using data from the X-ray crystallography studies of Rosalind Franklin and Maurice Wilkins at King's College London.

A double-stranded life

DNA has a **double helix** form comprising two strands of linked subunits called nucleotides. Each nucleotide is made up of a sugar, a phosphate and one of four bases – adenine (A), thymine (T), guanine (G) and cytosine (C). The order of bases on a single strand of DNA is effectively a recipe for making proteins, which in turn make cells, tissues and whole organisms. The bases on opposing strands of DNA pair up in a consistent order (A with T and C with G) and this pairing rule means that when separated, each strand of a DNA molecule can act as a template for assembling a copy of the other.

The copying process can be repeated endlessly and the copy is almost always perfect. Very occasionally, an error or **mutation** occurs. Many mutations make no difference to the function of the gene, but some will change it, producing genetic variation and hence the raw material for evolution by natural selection (see p. 44).

(see p. 44)

QUICK FACT

Watson, Crick and Wilkins received Nobel Prizes in 1962 for their work on DNA, an honour Franklin missed out on, having died of ovarian cancer at just 37.

Marvellous mammals

Mammals first appeared on Earth about 240 million years ago, but for much of this time they were small, unassuming creatures, similar to modern tree shrews. They came into their own at the demise of the dinosaurs, rapidly diversifying to become the ecologically dominant life form on Earth.

Mammals are united by a common strategy for feeding their young, and the clue is in the name. Every young mammal, be it a human or hyena, whale or wombat, is given a nutritional kick-start of milk, produced in **mammary glands**.

As a general rule mammals are also furry or hairy, though in some species, including humans and cetaceans (whales and dolphins), this trait is reduced.

MAMMAL
MILK BAR

Come and warm up

Mammals are **homeothermic**, which means they are warm-blooded and capable of maintaining a constant body temperature, optimised for all the chemical reactions that sustain active life. This gives mammals (and birds, which are also homeothermic) a physical and mental edge over species that operate at ambient temperatures, especially in more extreme conditions. It's an energetically expensive strategy, though, so some species are able to down-regulate their internal thermostats during hibernation or torpor as a means of saving energy.

Do you take milk?

Lactation is rather odd. In evolutionary terms, it began as a means of preventing porous eggs drying out – a greasy substance not unlike sweat was secreted from glands in the mother's underside as she brooded. Newly hatched young could gain nutritional benefit from licking this greasy substance from her fur. Modern egg-laying mammals (echidnas and the duck-billed platypus) lack teats – the milk just leaks from glands on the female's belly and her babies slurp it up. The specialised delivery system of teats or nipples came later. The chief benefit of this elaborate system is that the young have an immediate source of food, and can be protected from fluctuations in resources. As a result, mammals are able to exploit a wide variety of habitats.

QUICK FACT

There are 21 orders of mammals including rodents, cetaceans, marsupials, primates and bats, totalling about 5,500 species.

QUICK FACT

In most, but not all, mammal species, females give birth to live young – the exceptions are the monotremes, which lay rubbery eggs.

MILK

Renewable energy → → → → →

Burning fossil fuels, or harvesting the energy of radioactive decay, is a one-time deal, because the energy sources are destroyed in the process. Renewable energy sources are naturally replenished – immediately in the case of solar radiation, or over a few months or years for biofuels.

Apart from the obvious truth that Earth's finite resources, such as oil, coal, gas and nuclear fuels, will run out some day, renewables have the advantage of being cleaner at the point of use. On the downside they are polluting to construct, costly in terms of both energy and cash, they take up a lot of space, impact on wildlife, and can be visually intrusive. All of which applies to non-renewables too, of course.

Going green – types of renewable energy

Solar thermal Sunshine heats water, which is then used directly for domestic or commercial heating.

Concentrated solar power (CSP) Sunlight is focused by mirrors into a high-energy beam, which is used to drive a heat engine generator.

Photovoltaic (PV) solar The PV cells that make up solar panels are made from photovoltaic semiconductor materials such as silicon. The flow of electrons emitted when they absorb light energy forms the basis of an electric current.

Hydro Water flowing down a gradient can be used to spin turbines and generate electricity on a small, medium or vast scale.

Wind In wind farms, the turbines are faced into the wind to maximise output, but have to be shut down in a gale to avoid damage.

Wave A variety of devices, including hydraulic rams, turbines and linear motors, have been invented to convert wave energy into electricity.

Tidal Tides are created by the gravitational pull of the sun and moon on the world's oceans. Electricity can be generated by turbine-alternators strategically placed in fast-moving tidal races.

Geothermal Heat from deep inside the Earth's crust is used to create steam to drive electricity generators. Geothermally heated water can also be used directly in central heating.

Biofuels Organic material can be burned in the same way as coal to make steam to power generators. Biofuels include fast-growing plants such as elephant grass and willow; other sources include dung and organic refuse.

Bright sparks

In 1839, French physicist Edmond Becquerel discovered certain materials produced small amounts of electric current when exposed to light. In 1905 Albert Einstein explained this photoelectric effect, which became the basis for photovoltaic cells used in solar panels.

Renewables currently contribute about 20 per cent of global energy consumption and electricity generation. These are the world's largest renewable energy plants in different categories.

2,400MW*
Wave Orkney Wave Power Station, Scotland

300MW*
Tidal Wando Hoenggan Waterway, Korea

392MW
Solar Ivanpah Solar Electric Generating System, Mojave Desert, California

550MW
Biomass Oy Alholmens Kraft Power Station, Finland

630MW
Wind (offshore) London Array, England

6,000MW*
Wind (onshore) Gansu Wind Farm, China

1,000MW
Geothermal The Geysers Geothermal Field, California

22,000MW
Hydro Three Gorges Dam, China

FOR COMPARISON
Typical nuclear power station: about 1,000MW
Typical coal-fired station: 500MW
MW = megawatt

* Predicted outputs – these plants are still under construction

51

Tolerable temperatures

Life as we know it is extraordinarily picky about temperature, and could only have evolved on what astronomers call a 'Goldilocks planet' – not too hot, and not too cold.

Ahhh, that's just right

The human body is exceptionally sensitive to temperature. Your body operates at 37° Celsius – shift this a couple of degrees in either direction and you'll feel rough. More than five degrees and chances are you'd be decidedly dead. However, as a homeotherm you're able to use a range of physiological and behavioural tricks to maintain a constant body temperature across a range of ambient conditions. An appropriately dressed human can tolerate ambient temperatures from in the region of -20 to 35°C. Our technological advancement makes us one of the most thermally flexible species on the planet.

It's chilly out

So-called **extremophile** organisms cope with temperatures much cooler and much warmer than we do. Many species of amphibian, fish and insect survive sub-zero temperatures by producing antifreeze chemicals in their blood. Larvae of the Alaskan red flat bark beetle tolerate -150°C and the tiny and exceptionally weird aquatic creatures known as tardigrades have survived being experimentally frozen at -272°C, a shade above absolute zero, the coldest temperature possible.

141,700,000,000,000,000,000,000,000,000,000°C
Temperature of the universe immediately after the Big Bang

 10,000,000,000,000°C
Heat of lead ion collisions in the CERN Large Hadron Collider

 350,000,000,000°C
Heat generated by merging neutron stars

 16,000,000°C The centre of the Sun

28,000°C Bolt of lightning

5,500°C Surface temperature of the Sun

100°C Boiling temperature of water

70.7°C Hottest recorded air temperature, Lut Desert, Iran

37°C Human body temperature

0°C Freezing point of water

-93.2°C The coldest air temperature recorded on Earth – at 81.8 degrees South and 59.3 degrees East in Antarctica

 -273.15°C Absolute zero – the coldest temperature theoretically possible anywhere in the Universe

Phew, it's hot

At the other extreme, desert ants routinely go about their business at 60°C, communities of specialist marine crustaceans, molluscs and polychaete worms living in the vicinity of hydrothermal vents tolerate water temperatures of 80°C, while so-called **thermophilic** bacteria inhabiting hot springs thrive at 100°C and above.

Temperature scales

❄

Temperature is usually measured in degrees **Celsius**, though scientists often refer to **Kelvin** – which is the same scale, but shifted just over 273 degrees so that absolute zero is 0°K. Just three countries – Belize, Myanmar and the USA – now officially currently use the **Fahrenheit** scale, in which water freezes at 32°F and boils at 212°F.

Here comes the Sun

The apparent passage of the Sun across the sky follows a pattern as regular as clockwork – which is to say that clockwork strives to match the regularity of the Sun. So it's no surprise that we are not the only species that uses solar cues for time and date.

Have you got the time?

Humans have used **sundials** and **solar calendars** to tell time and date for millennia. The principle of a sundial is that the shadow of an upright (called the *gnomon*) moves predictably as the Earth turns under the Sun. A solar calendar relies on the fact that the Sun appears to return to the same position at a given time (usually noon or dawn) on the same date each year as Earth completes its annual orbit. The movement of the Earth around the Sun, and the angle at which it is tilted, also influence the duration of daylight hours on a given date. Only on the equator are days and night always equal. Elsewhere, the seasons are marked by predictable changes in day length, known as **photoperiod**.

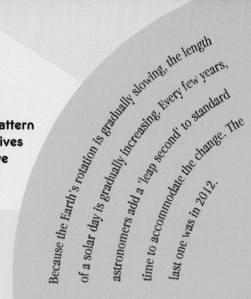

Because the Earth's rotation is gradually slowing, the length of a solar day is gradually increasing. Every few years, astronomers add a 'leap second' to standard time to accommodate the change. The last one was in 2012.

Sundials

A simple sundial can be fashioned from a stick pushed into the ground, but to be accurate the gnomon should point north and be oriented at the same angle as the axis of rotation of the Earth. Achieving this is tricky, as both angles vary with location. It's also worth remembering that local solar time varies from standard time depending on where the location is within a time zone – solar noon in Lowestoft, for example, is 7 minutes ahead of Greenwich Mean Time (also known as Coordinated Universal Time or UTC) and in Penzance it is about 22 minutes behind GMT. Then there are adjustments for daylight saving. All in all, the invention of the clock and the watch saved a whole lot of hassle.

That was good timing

Many animals appear to have an innate perception of photoperiod, which allows amazing feats of timekeeping, such as arriving at breeding grounds or moulting to a new coat of winter white on more or less the same date each year. In other seasonal behaviours, such as hibernation and breeding, timing may also be influenced by factors such as temperature and food availability.

Time to shine

Some plants use photoperiod to tell them when to flower. Long-day species bloom in late spring or early summer, while short-day species only begin to develop flowers when the hours of darkness increase above a threshold, usually in late summer. Short-day species can be prevented from flowering by being exposed to a short flash of light during the night.

Very like a whale: cloud classification

Who hasn't gazed up at a cloud and seen distinctive shapes such as mountains or animal forms? The basic cloud classifications were thought up by British amateur meteorologist Luke Howard in 1803 and continue to be used worldwide.

Cirrus Hairlike wisps of high cloud, very white in daylight but may take on fantastic colours at sunrise and sunset.

Height at base: 5,500–12,000m

Cirrostratus Very thin, high clouds often blanketing huge areas, sometimes almost completely transparent so sunlight can still form shadows. Often cause a halo effect around the sun (or moon).

Height at base: 5,500–12,000m

Altocumulus Clumps of white or grey mid-level clouds, one side of which will be shaded according to the direction of the sun.

Height at base: 600–5,500m

Stratus The lowest of clouds, uniform and grey – at ground level we call them mist or fog. They may produce drizzle.

Height at base: 0–2,000m

Stratocumulus Common, well-defined low clouds with flattened bases. They can be well spaced, or linked together. Often with several variable shades of white to dark grey in one cloud.

Height at base: 350–2,000m

Nimbostratus Thick layers of uniform mid-level cloud – makers of the classic 'grey day'. Often the source of steady rain or snow.

Height at base: 600–3,000m

Cirrocumulus Also known as a mackerel sky because the patterns of cloudlets can resemble the streaky flanks of a mackerel. Cloudlets comprise ice crystals rather than water vapour.

Height at base: 2,000–12,000m

Altostratus Thin, high, typically grey clouds made up of ice and water droplets. Sometimes the sun can be seen through the cloud, but not enough light passes through to create shadows.

Height at base: 2,100–5,500m

Cumulus Classic fluffy white clouds like you used to draw as a kid. Usually white and cauliflower-like on top, sometimes grey at the bottom – can produce rain.

Height at base: 350–2,000m

Cumulonimbus Very tall clouds, often with a distinctive flat, anvil-shaped head. From a distance they might resemble pillars or mountains. Associated with heavy rain, hail, thunder, lightning and other extreme weather such as tornadoes.

Height at base: 335–2,000m

Candy floss Erm, this one is actually candy floss.

57

A cloud in a bottle

You'll be used to hearing weather forecasters refer to high and low pressures and their associated weather – high pressure generally brings clear, dry conditions and low pressure overcast or wet weather. But how does pressure make a difference?

You will need

- A 2-litre plastic drink bottle, with the labels removed so you can see what's going on inside
- A bottle of isopropyl cleaning or rubbing alcohol*
- A bicycle pump or gym ball pump (the kind that looks like a big plastic syringe work well)
- Vaseline
- Safety specs

1 Specs on! Trickle a little alcohol into the bottle – 5–10ml is plenty. Now smear the opening with Vaseline and insert the pump into the neck so that it seals.

2 Pump air into the bottle until you feel firm resistance. You will need to hold the pump in place to keep the seal. Watch carefully what happens in the bottle when you release the seal by removing the pump.

3 Once you've got the hang of making clouds, try dispelling them by replacing the pump and raising the pressure again.

Warning Please, don't be silly enough to try and breathe the cloud – pure alcohol is nasty stuff.

If only changing the real weather was this easy!

PUMP!

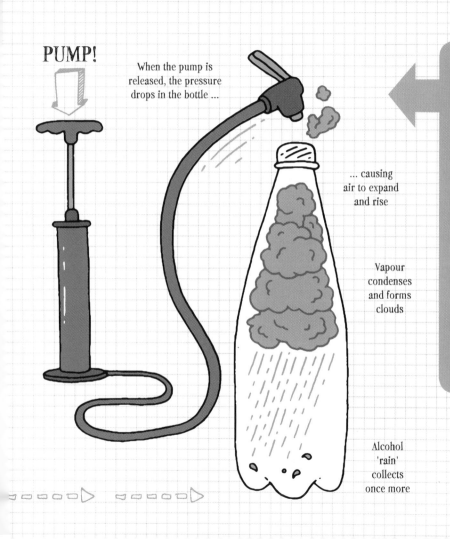

When the pump is released, the pressure drops in the bottle ...

... causing air to expand and rise

Vapour condenses and forms clouds

Alcohol 'rain' collects once more

What's happening?

Air contains water vapour as a result of evaporation from the surface of the Earth – this is the **humidity** you'll also hear meteorologists talking about. In your bottle, the humidity is created by alcohol vapour. When pressure drops, air expands and rises, leading to a cooling effect and causing vapour to condense into tiny droplets, forming clouds. When these droplets reach a certain size where gravity can overcome the rising air, they fall as drizzle, rain or snow.

* Alcohol is used for this experiment because it evaporates more quickly and easily than water and thus makes a more dramatic cloud effect. For a more faithful recreation of cloud formation, however, you can perform the same experiment using warm water.

Wacky weather!

We're obsessed with the weather, and with climate change set to bring increasingly extreme events, you can expect many of these records to fall in future years...

'Extreme weather' is a relative term, meteorologically speaking, used to describe conditions out of the ordinary for the location and time of year. For example, on 10 August 2003, thermometers in Kent registered 38°C – an extreme, record-breaking temperature for the UK maybe, but refreshing by equatorial standards.

Parts of the Atacama Desert in Chile experienced no rain for 400 years between 1571 and 1971.

The heaviest hailstone fell in Gopalganj, Bangladesh, in April 1986. It weighed 1.02kg.

The largest hailstone fell in Vivian, South Dakota, in July 2010. It measured 20cm across and 47.3cm in circumference.

Most rainfall ...
- *in one minute* 38mm, in Barot, Guadeloupe; November 1970
- *in one hour* 305mm, in Holt, Missouri, USA; June 1947
- *in 24 hours* 1825mm, on Reunion Island, January 1966 (Cyclone Denise)
- *in one year* 26,470mm, in Meghalaya, India; 1860–61

On 26 March 1987 a $78 million NASA rocket called Atlas-Centaur was struck nine times by lightning, seconds after lift-off. It exploded over the Atlantic, along with a further £83 million worth of military satellite hardware. Oops.

Hurricane, cyclone or typhoon?

Actually they are regional names for the same thing – rotating storm systems, originating in the tropics, in which sustained wind speeds build to over 119km/h. They're generally known as hurricanes in the north Atlantic and northeast Pacific, typhoons in the northwest Pacific and cyclones in the south Pacific and Indian Oceans.

Globally, lightning strikes on average about 50 times every second of every day.

The strongest recorded gust of wind topped 408km/h during Cyclone Olivia on Barrow Island, Western Australia, in 1996.

The deadliest storm on record was the Great Bhola Cyclone, Bangladesh, 1970. While only a Category 3 storm, the resulting storm surge caused the deaths of 300,000–500,000 people living on the low-lying Ganges Delta.

The fastest of all winds on Earth happen inside short-lived tornadoes, but are difficult to measure with accuracy. The fastest on record is a three-second gust inside a tornado at Bridge Creek, Oklahoma, in 1999. It was recorded at 484km/h using a Doppler radar device.

The most lightning-prone places on Earth are Catatumbo River, Venezuela, and Kifuka in the Democratic Republic of Congo. Both receive tens of thousands of strikes a year.

The strongest sustained winds came with Typhoon Haiyan, a Category 5 tropical cyclone that struck the Philippines in 2013. Wind speeds of 315km/h were maintained for more than a minute.

Perceptive plants

Next time you mow the lawn, lean on a tree, admire a floral display or munch into an apple, a chip or a carrot, consider this – plants don't have brains, but they certainly do have feelings.

Plants see

Anyone who grows a pot plant on a windowsill will know that it perceives light and grows towards it. Sunflowers are named for their habit of tracking the sun across the sky, and in the northern hemisphere the distinct sun-ward southern tilt of trees growing in the open has been used for centuries as a natural aid to navigation. The tilt in the southern hemisphere is to the north.

Plants smell and taste

Plants are highly sensitive to a wide variety of chemicals in air, soil and water. The shoots of dodder, a parasitic plant, even know the difference between tender tomato plants and tough wheat – they will always grow towards their preferred host species.

Plants feel

Climbing plants such as peas and bindweed have tendrils or stems that coil on contact with a suitable support, and some can sense a touch considerably lighter than that picked up by our own fingers. The West Indian gherkin, a type of cucumber, can sense a thread weighing 0.25g – with eyes closed, most people require a thread laid over their fingers to weigh at least 2g before they sense it.

Plants know where they are!

When a seed germinates, it invariably sends shoots *up*, while roots go *down*. This innate gravity sense is achieved using tiny starchy granules called statocysts, which drop to the bottom of gravity-sensing cells, and the ability persists in mature plants – a tree knocked onto its side will make an abrupt switch and kink upwards once again, and a seedling turned upside down will make a U-turn.

Plants remember

You can trick a touch-me-not mimosa plant or a Venus flytrap into closing, just by touching the leaves – but if you repeat the stimulus too often the plant will learn to ignore you.

Plants communicate ... and manipulate!

When a plant is infected by parasites or disease, or attacked by herbivores, it will release chemicals that warn its neighbours of the threat. These chemicals trigger other plants to produce defensive chemicals such as bitter-tasting tannins to deter leaf-munchers. Plants also go to enormous lengths to attract pollinators and seed dispersers – the appearance and scent of flowers and fruits are advertisements, and the sweetness of nectar and fruit sugars are bribes.

Crikey! What's happening to you?

What seeds need

Packed tightly into every seed is the embryo of a new life and a parcel of energy to sustain it through the first few weeks of growth until it can produce food for itself. To trigger the everyday mini-miracle of germination, just add water.

You will need

- Three transparent plastic takeaway boxes with lids
- Kitchen towel
- Mung beans (or other sprouting beans); these are available from large supermarkets and wholefood retailers*
- Water
- Bradawl or sharp skewer
- Cling film
- Shoe box or similar cardboard box

① Rinse and dry the takeaway boxes and fold one sheet of kitchen paper into the bottom of each.

② Add about 2 tbsp of water to each box. The exact amount doesn't matter, but to be scientific about it you should use the same quantity in each, so use the same spoon for measuring.

③ Next add 10 beans to each box, and fit the lid. Using the bradawl or skewer, carefully make about 20 holes in the lids of TWO boxes. Put the same number in each.

④ Place all three boxes on a bright windowsill. Cover one of the pierced-lid boxes with the upturned shoebox to exclude most of the light. Leave for four days.

* The beansprouts you get from this experiment won't be great for eating – but a packet will contain plenty of spares that you can cultivate according to the instructions on the pack, which will involve repeated soaking and rinsing. The result will be exceptionally nutritious and delicious; just make sure you buy those clearly marked as suitable for sprouting. Those sold in garden centres etc. for planting will probably have been treated with pesticides and should not be eaten.

At the end of the experiment, open up your boxes and compare the sprouted beans inside. How long are the sprouts? What colour are they? Do they have leaves as well as roots? How do they respond to restricted air circulation or darkness?

If you have more boxes and windowsill space, you might try further variations on the experiment – checking the beans after more or less sprouting time, or giving them salt water instead of fresh.

Ripening fruit

This age-old kitchen trick is not only convenient for chefs, domestic cooks and the global produce trade – it is also evidence of an extraordinary plant strategy for survival.

You will need
- Two hard, unripe fruits – pears, avocados, plums or green tomatoes work well
- Two paper bags
- One really ripe banana

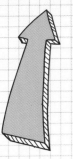

(1) Place the hard fruits into the bags, and add the banana to one of them. Scrunch down the top of each bag to seal it, and place both bags in a warm, dry place such as a windowsill.

(2) Check the condition of the fruit inside every day, resealing the bags each time. Which ripens first?

How does it work?
The ripe banana produces a chemical called ethylene, which functions as a plant hormone. Minute quantities of it in the atmosphere trigger a reaction that softens the flesh of unripe fruits and turns the starch they store into tempting sugars.

It's not just bananas that produce ethylene – all ripe fruits do it. For a plant, coordinated ripening increases the chances of seed dispersal, as a bunch of ripe fruit is more likely to attract a fruit-eating animal than a single one. Interestingly, damaged fruits also release lots of ethylene, so cut or bruised fruits also accelerate the ripening – and rotting – of their neighbours. So there is plenty of truth in the old adage that it only takes one bad apple to spoil a boxful of 'keepers'. But the effect can also be put to good use – ancient Egyptian farmers knew that slashing one fig in a bunch could make the others ripen faster.

The process also works with ethylene from other sources – Chinese farmers used to ripen pears in sheds filled with incense smoke, which, it turns out, also contains ethylene.

Did you know?

These days ethylene gas is used to ripen fruit after shipping – allowing some produce to be carried by sea while still green instead of having to be picked ripe and rushed to its destination by air. This is one of the factors that gives bananas a surprisingly low (for exotic fruit) carbon footprint.

QUICK FACT

Ethylene is the same molecule found in polythene.

For me?

Colour my world

In mammals, full colour vision is limited to primates, including humans, and some marsupials. Our ability evolved as an adaptation to a fruit-eating diet – and to a clever plant strategy making sure we only picked and ate fruits when the seeds were mature and ready for dispersal. So in a way, the world of colour we enjoy is the result of plants manipulating our behaviour.

Pollination

Pollination is the delivery of pollen from the male anther of one flowering plant to the female part, or stigma, of another. And Nature has devised a wide range of mechanisms for allowing this to happen.

A **pollen** grain is a delivery module for **male gametes** – the plant equivalent of sperm – helping them reach a female **ovule**, which is typically embedded in a part of the flower called the carpel, or on the scales of a cone. Each grain contains two gametes, and it takes both to 'double fertilise' an ovule, forming the two components of a seed – the embryo and its surrounding endosperm. The latter contains the energy required for germination (and is the reason seeds are so nutritious).

Gone with the wind

Plants use a variety of methods to ensure pollination. Conifers, grasses and catkin-bearing trees such as hazel and birch rely on the wind to spread a fine mist of pollen far and wide – this is the stuff responsible for hay fever.

FREE NECTAR!

Precious dust

Pollen is easily preserved, and under a microscope the grains of different species can be quite distinctive – some resemble tennis balls, hamburgers, naval mines and even the Death Star from *Star Wars*. These characteristics form the basis of the science of pollen **palynology** – literally the 'analysis of dust'. Pollen analysis has become a frequently used tool in archaeology, climatology and forensic science.

A little help from my friends

Most plants take a more targeted approach, enlisting the help of animal pollinators. These include a huge array of insects – bees, of course, but also flies, butterflies and moths, and beetles. **Nectar** is an inducement – a sugary reward that tempts pollinators to enter the flower – and the colour, structure and scent of flowers are advertisements. Many plants tailor their flower to one particular pollinator species – this kind of loyalty increases the chances of pollen being delivered to another plant of the same species. Larger animals can also be pollinators – the long beak and hovering flight of hummingbirds is an adaptation to nectar-feeding, while certain bats perform the same service at night. Plants pollinated by bats and nocturnal moths flower at night and tend to advertise with large, pale flowers and far-carrying scents.

All strategies for **cross-pollination** are risky, and some plants opt for the sure-fire strategy of **self-pollination**. Self-pollination does rule out the chance for healthy mixing of the gene pool. But it's better than not reproducing at all.

69

Seed bombing

Psst ... Fancy a bit of guerrilla gardening? The idea behind seed bombs is that you lob one into an unloved or ecologically barren corner and saunter away feeling smug and slightly rebellious, leaving sun, rain and time to do the rest.

You know that place that no one seems to look after? The vacant plot, the sterile grassy roundabout, the car park edge, the bin alley? Unloved and unsightly scraps of land are everywhere. But Nature doesn't care much what they look like, and given half a chance she can transform them into something wonderful. Plenty of native wildflowers are actually very well adapted to exposed 'wasteland' conditions. The 'recipe' here should make about 40 bombs.

You will need

- 500g potter's clay powder
- 100g well-rotted compost
- 50g wildflower seed
- Water to mix

1) Mix the clay and compost in a large bowl, and water very gradually, mixing as you go. When you have a firm dough, divide it into as many chunks as you have seed varieties.

2) Mix seeds of one species into each portion, and divide as necessary to make individual bombs about the size and shape of a conker.

3) Leave to dry in a warm place until hard.

Woo hooooo!

Please only use native seeds, not imported or cultivated varieties. Try herb Robert, red campion, oxeye daisy, knapweed, forget-me-not and common poppy. You can also throw in the odd sunflower – they're not native, but birds will appreciate the seeds.

Use powdered potter's clay rather than something you've dug up – you want to be sure the only seeds in your bomb are the ones you intend to be there, and avoid spreading an invasive species such as Himalayan balsam or Japanese knotweed. Likewise, if you're using home-made compost, make sure it's well rotted and dried so you can be confident it doesn't contain viable garden or culinary seed.

If you like, you can include a mixture of seed types together in each ball, but bear in mind you'll be setting them up in direct competition with each other and some species do much better on their own until well established.

(4) It's time to release your bombs. They're the ideal size to chuck over a fence or out of a window. Use several per site, as germination rates can be quite low. If you've made them well, the bombs will protect the seeds from scavenging animals while they gradually absorb water and begin to germinate.

Happy bombing!

Photosynthesis – the key to life

Photosynthesis is the means by which plants make food – not just for themselves, but for almost every living organism on the planet.

Nature's mini factories

Chloroplasts are tiny green units of plant cells that contain the pigment **chlorophyll**, and they are the structures where water and carbon dioxide are combined in a reaction powered by sunlight to make the simple sugar **glucose**. This product can be stored as starch or used directly as a source of chemical energy for growth, flowering or the production of spores, seeds or fruits. Chlorophyll facilitates the complex chemical reaction of photosynthesis. It contains hydrogen, carbon and oxygen, as well as nitrate and magnesium, which plants extract from nutrients in the soil, along with water. Photosynthesis produces a waste product, a gas that diffuses out of leaves in such quantity that it permeates the global atmosphere. This gas is oxygen. So it's no exaggeration to say we rely on plants for every breath we take.

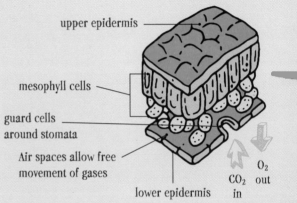

LEAF SECTION

upper epidermis

mesophyll cells

guard cells around stomata

Air spaces allow free movement of gases

lower epidermis

O_2 out

CO_2 in

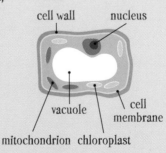

CELL

cell wall

nucleus

vacuole

cell membrane

mitochondrion   chloroplast

The gases involved in photosynthesis pass in and out of the leaf via tiny openings called **stomata**. They're usually on the shady underside to reduce the amount of water lost by evaporation.

Sunlight & CO$_2$

LEAF

CHLOROPLAST

Inside the double membrane of the chloroplast, membranous structures called thylakoids are usually arranged on top of one another in stacks called grana. The thylakoids contain chlorophyll and are where photosynthesis actually happens.

Why are plants green?

White light is actually a mixture of rainbow colours – what we call the visible spectrum. Plants look green because photosynthesis is driven mostly by blue and red light. The chlorophyll in plant cells absorbs these required wavelengths from sunlight and reflects the green – which is then picked up by our eyes.

Flower power

Flowers are styled by Nature (or rather by natural selection) to be noticed. Their eye-catching colours, varied and intricate structures and arresting scents exist for exactly that purpose, although the show is not intended for us, but for an army of pollinators.

Rafflesia arnoldii produces the largest individual bloom of any flowering plant, at up to 1m across and weighing 11kg. It's no beauty though, and its scent resembles that of decaying flesh – hence its common name, 'corpse flower'.

The titan arum produces the largest unbranched **inflorescence** of any flowering plant, at up to 3.1m high. Confusingly, it is also known as corpse flower, on account of its putrid scent, despite being unrelated to *Rafflesia*.

The 'Tulip Mania' of the 17th century centred on Dutch flower markets where single bulbs sold for more than their weight in gold.

The first plant to flower in space was *Arabidopsis* – a species of rock cress grown in a lab aboard the Soviet space station Salyut 7 in 1982.

Bamboo plants usually reproduce vegetatively, with single plants able to spread over decades to form entire bamboo forests. Eventually, however, after anything from 40–130 years, all plants from the same stock (including those removed and planted anywhere else in the world) will flower simultaneously, then die.

The tallest sunflower was grown by Hans-Peter Schiffer in Germany in 2014. It measured 9.17m high.

The flowers and leaves of the gas plant, or burning bush, exude highly flammable volatile oils – a single match held nearby can ignite the whole plant in a flash.

Some plants, such as the Amazon water lily and cuckoo pint, are **thermogenic** – they produce heat as an added attraction for pollinators.

Every year in Japan, festivals and open-air parties are held to celebrate the cherry blossom season. The practice is known as *hanami*.

One of the world's most expensive spices, saffron, comes from crocus flowers. The stigmas and styles are collected and dried, then used to flavour and impart a rich yellow colour to foods such as rice.

Bulbophyllum nocturnum, discovered in 2011, is the first known night-flowering orchid. The blooms last only a few hours – and initially botanists could not work out why promising-looking buds always seemed to wither and die. Flowering was only observed when a researcher took a specimen home for the night.

The smallest flower is produced, naturally enough, by the smallest flowering plant – an aquatic duckweed called *Wolffia*, also known as watermeal.

Plant pigments

Ever made the mistake of eating spaghetti Bolognese while wearing a white shirt? Nothing stains quite as well as a good rich sauce made with olive oil and tomatoes. But why is that, when pure tomato juice washes out quite easily? This experiment examines the properties of plant pigments; you can use tomatoes or carrots.

You will need

- 4 jam jars with lids
- A large carrot, or the skins of 6 large, dark-red tomatoes*
- Light-coloured cooking oil (groundnut or grapeseed are usually palest)
- Water
- Tea strainer

* To peel tomatoes easily, put them in a large bowl and cover them with boiling water for about 60 seconds first.

1 Use a fine grater to shred the carrot. Or, if you're using tomato skins, chop them finely. Divide the shredded carrot or tomato skins in two and put each half into a separate jar.

2 Add 50ml water to one jar, and 50ml oil to the other. Screw on the lids and shake for 30 seconds. Using a clean tea strainer, filter the carrot/tomato water into a clean jar.

3 Then wash and carefully dry the tea strainer and repeat using the carrot/tomato oil (this will take longer to drain – leave it for a few minutes).

4 Now you'll have two preparations – one containing pigments that are water-soluble, the other containing those that are lipid (fat)-soluble. How do the colours compare? To prove the point, add some clean oil to the jar with carrot/tomato water and about the same amount of clean water to the carrot/tomato oil. Can you get any of the pigment from the watery solution to mix with the oil? Or the oil pigments to enter the water?

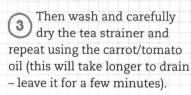

But what about my shirt?

Going back to those Bolognese stains. The culprit there is a pigment called lycopene – abundant in tomatoes and a valuable antioxidant. The reason lycopene stains are so stubborn on clothing and plastic is that lycopene is lipid-soluble. Scrubbing with water and detergent won't break it down. Fortunately a little bit of sunshine will – the pigment degrades quickly in UV, so wash or wet down those stained items and leave them in the sun to bleach naturally – no nasty chemicals required.

Tremendous trees

There's no doubting it, whether from a scientific, artistic, spiritual, engineering or commercial perspective, trees are cool. Few other organisms can match them for beauty, scale, longevity and ecological and practical value.

What makes a tree a tree?

A tree (if there was any doubt) is a long-lived (perennial) plant with an elongated woody stem (a trunk). Most are relatively large, but low-growing forms do occur, especially in exposed locations where conditions make lofty growth impossible.

Record breakers

The tallest tree currently living is a coastal redwood called Hyperion, which stands 115.55m tall, and is thought to be about 800 years old. Its precise location in northern California is a closely guarded secret.

The oldest tree of known age is a bristlecone pine, also at a secret location in California, confirmed as 5,064 years old in 2013 from analysis of a core sample. A number of European yews, including several in British churchyards, are estimated to be of a similar age but this cannot be confirmed because their cores have long since rotted out. The oldest planted tree is a sacred fig, Jaya Sri Maha Bodhi, supposedly seeded from the original Bodhi tree under which Lord Buddha gained Enlightenment. The young tree was planted in Anuradhapura, Sri Lanka, and is still there, 2,303 years later.

Going around in circles

Trees live in four dimensions – the fourth being time. An oak might easily live for a thousand years, and our most ancient yews pre-date recorded history in Europe. Trees may not be able to talk, but they can yield historical information – in particular relating to climate. The annual rings laid down in the trunk timbers of trees record the stop-start sequence of growth – a spurt in the summer and a period of inactivity in winter. The growth achieved in a given year is indicated by the thickness of the ring – so the sequence of good, bad and indifferent summers can be read like a barcode. The study of tree rings can be used to date a section of trunk even if its origins are unknown. The technique is used to date old buildings from their structural timbers.

Dating a tree by its rings is called dendrochronology.

Leaf rubbing

A delightfully straightforward art project, leaf rubbing is also a great way to investigate the structure and function of leaves.

You will need

- A selection of leaves – ideally well-developed late summer or autumn windfalls that still have some flexibility (dry, crispy leaves are no good – they'll just disintegrate)
- A flat, smooth surface
- A few sheets of plain, smooth-textured paper – standard copier paper is ideal
- Wax crayons in whatever colours take your fancy

1) Arrange your first leaf upside down on the smooth surface (so the bumpy veins on its underside face up).

2) Cover with the paper and use a crayon to rub back and forth over the leaf. Take the colour just past the leaf edge so that you pick out its shape as well as the pattern of veins. Repeat with as many leaves and colours as you wish.

3) For a variation, you can paint over rubbings made with light-coloured crayons or even candle wax with thin, water-based paint or watery ink – the paint will only colour the unwaxed part of the page, making the rubbing stand out clearly.

Turn over a new leaf

The shape of leaves and the pattern of veins is useful in plant taxonomy – try to identify those you use. Examine the difference between the broad leaves and branching venation of **dicotyledons**, such as oak or sycamore, and the almost parallel venation of **monocotyledons** like grasses and palms.

For non-flowering plants like ferns, the intricacy of their branching structure will help you identify them: are they pinnate (with leafy lobes called pinnules branching once off the central stem of a frond), bipinnate (with miniature fronds branching off bigger fronds) or even tripinnate (frondlets off mini-fronds off big fronds)?

Striving in vein

The veins in leaves are not like the veins of animals, though they do perform a transport role.

In fact, each vein is a bundle of vessels of two main types: **xylem**, which transport water, and **phloem**, which carry sugars and other nutrients from the leaves to other parts of the plant. Each vein is protected by a layer of tough bundle sheath cells.

Let's eat!

The need to consume food for energy and nutrients (as opposed to manufacturing it as plants do) is one of the key characteristics of animals. A food web is a convenient means of describing the complex and rather brutal business of who eats who.

A tangled web

We sometimes talk of food chains, as though the flow of energy from one level to the next – for example, pondweed, tadpole, duckling, pike – is rather simple. Which, of course, it's not. Most animals eat more than one type of food, and most plants and prey animals are eaten by more than one consumer.

Where do you get your energy?

Most food webs are ultimately based on **producers** or **autotrophs**

– organisms that are able to manufacture sugars. These are mostly plants, but also include some bacteria. Everything else is a **consumer**, or **heterotroph**. Much of the energy an animal consumes is burned up in the process of staying alive – only a limited amount is conserved or converted to living tissue. Thus it takes a lot of producers to sustain a primary consumer. Carnivores, and in particular top predators, are naturally rare. The same logic tells us that as

the planet's most avid and wide-ranging consumers, sustainable living means eating less meat and more plant material.

That's my favourite!

Most animals have some level of food specialism, dictated by the food they are physically able to obtain and process. Even omnivores, which have a broad, mixed diet, are limited to some extent. **Carnivores** eat mostly meat: some are predators, while

FOOD WEB

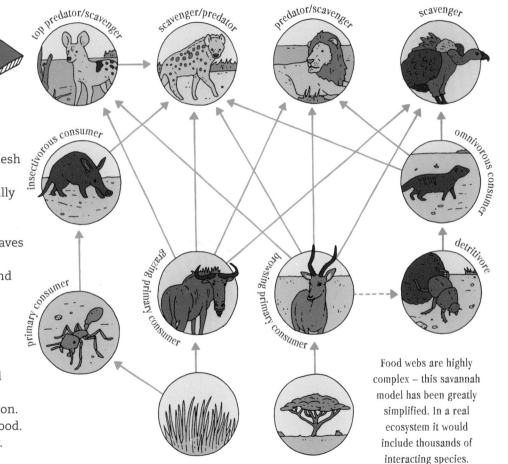

others scavenge dead flesh or carrion.

Herbivores are principally vegetarian; grazers specialise in grass and herbs; browsers take leaves and shoots.

Detritivores eat dead and decaying material.

Granivores eat seeds.

Frugivores eat fruit.

Piscivores prefer fish.

Insectivores eat insects and other small invertebrates.

Planktivores eat plankton.

Sanguinivores drink blood.

Nectarivores sip nectar.

top predator/scavenger

scavenger/predator

predator/scavenger

scavenger

insectivorous consumer

omnivorous consumer

detritivore

primary consumer

grazing primary consumer

browsing primary consumer

Food webs are highly complex – this savannah model has been greatly simplified. In a real ecosystem it would include thousands of interacting species.

Where did he go? Animal camouflage

Now you see me, now you don't. Camouflage in animals evolved to give them protection when they need it most – which is usually when hunting, or being hunted.

Camouflage ranges from the basic – for example, the generic dowdy brown of many small mammals and songbirds – to the exquisite. The best is able to confound human vision.

Light and shade

Many aquatic animals, especially fish, exhibit **countershading** – a dark upper surface and a pale underside help them blend in with shadowy depths or a bright surface, depending whether they are seen from above or below. Some **bioluminescent** species, such as hatchetfish, emit light from their bellies that is the same blue as the sunlight filtering down from above, making them virtually invisible from below.

Blending in

Most camouflage works best against a particular type of background – coarse sand for a flounder, mossy trunks for the mossy-tailed gecko, grass for a grasshopper – but some rather unlikely-looking patterns work well simply by breaking up the animal's outline, for example a tiger's bold stripes.

All change

Some animals change their camouflage on a seasonal basis, for example, Arctic foxes and the grouse-like ptarmigan moult to a coat of winter white. Others change much faster: many fish and frogs darken or lighten their colouring to blend in with their backgrounds. A select group, including chameleons, octopuses and squid, are able to match the colour and texture of variable backgrounds with such speed and accuracy that they are effectively cloaked in invisibility.

So great is the control some of these animals have over the pigment-containing cells or **chromatophores** in their skin, they can use waves of colour change as a form of communication.

Spot the egg

It's not just animals that are camouflaged: the eggs of many ground-nesting birds are often mottled and streaked so they blend in with their surroundings.

Smells familiar

Camouflage doesn't have to be visual. Cuckoo wasps invade the nest burrows of other wasp species, eat their host's eggs or larvae and replace them with their own. Some are thought to release scents so similar to those of the host that in the darkness of the burrow, they are not recognised.

Animal tracking

It's exciting to discover a footprint in the mud or snow, a telltale sign that another creature recently crossed the same path you're taking. Every animal leaves a distinct trail or 'spoor' and, with practice, you can learn a lot about the species inhabiting an area.

You will need

- A field guide
- Nature journal, for taking notes and making drawings
- Magnifying lens
- Binoculars
- Camera
- Tape measure

(1) You will also need a suitable surface in which the tracks can be recorded. Fresh snow is the best medium of all, because it takes impressions well and covers everything – but you need to get out in it early before it starts to thaw or be trampled. Mud, silt, damp soil and sand can all be excellent surfaces, and even grass can be telling – look for trails in the dew and runways created where small mammals habitually travel.

(2) The best place to look for tracks is on existing trails at obvious crossing places and pinch-points – just like us, most animals will chose an easy route through cluttered habitat such as a woodland.

What to look for

• How big is the print? Measure it or photograph it alongside an object of known size, such as a coin, for scale.

• What shape is it overall – oval, round, heart-shaped or splayed like a starburst?

• How many toes can you see? Deer, sheep and cattle have two; dogs, foxes and cats have four; badgers, otters and bears have five. Rodents have four fingers and five toes. Birds have three forward-facing toes and sometimes an additional backward-facing one.

• Can you see claw marks? Squirrel, fox, badger and dog tracks show claws; feline prints don't.

• Are the front and back prints the same size? Prints that show small, round front feet and long back feet were probably left by a rabbit or hare.

• Is there any evidence of a dragging tail?

• What happens to the trail when it meets an obstacle such as a wall or fallen tree? This may give you an idea of the size and

agility of the animal. Many small animals like mice prefer to run in the shelter of a linear feature like a wall.

• Did the animal leap, pause or change direction at all? Why might this have been?

Unwelcome guests – parasites

Chances are by the end of this page you'll be itching and possibly not feeling like lunch. But don't let that put you off. Parasites are organisms that live at the expense of another living organism, the host, and they have some undeniably cool ways of doing so.

Loveable lice?

It's tempting to think of all parasites as malign, bent on causing death and disease. But in fact, killing the host and thereby dooming itself is the last thing a parasite wants to do. Indeed, many well-established host–parasite relationships become almost chummy, with the parasite taking no more than the host can spare.

Take the humble head louse – a parasite associated exclusively with human hosts. They love our clean, relatively thin hair, which is fairly easy to move about in, and spend their entire life cycle there, hatching from an egg or *nit*, feeding modestly on our blood, and occasionally taking the opportunity to move on when we put our heads together. They do no real harm and, next to other parasites, their habits seem almost wholesome.

My tummy hurts!

Problems come when a parasite infects a host to which it is less well adapted – such as the trypanosomes that cause sleeping sickness, or when the parasite's means of achieving transmission cause suffering in the host. Then we refer to the symptoms as parasitic disease.

Take the Guinea worm – a type of nematode. It requires two hosts to complete its life cycle – the first is a tiny aquatic crustacean known as a copepod, the second is a human. When the human ingests the copepod, along with unclean drinking water, the worm larvae it contains burrow into the

JUMP!

stomach lining, mature and mate. The fertilised female makes her way through the host's connective tissues to the skin, usually on the arms or legs, and emerges gradually from a painful blister. A natural reaction is to seek water to soothe the burning sensation. Immersion in water causes the female worm to release thousands of larvae, ready to be ingested by a copepod so the cycle can begin again. It's worked for thousands of years, but a rigorous programme of public education and water treatment means that the Guinea worm is well on its way to being eradicated.

Head louse experts have claimed that the popularity of 'selfies' may be increasing the incidence of head louse infestation in teenagers. However, this phenomenon has not been scientifically documented!

If only they could talk! Animal communication

Animals communicate in a wide variety of deliberate and involuntary ways – using scent, gesture, sound and many other means of signalling. And with practice it is possible for us to read the signals too.

?‡∫§&!#¿

Any dog or cat owner will tell you that species is no barrier to communication, and that animals readily express themselves, make demands and manipulate your behaviour – inviting a stroke or a tummy rub, begging to go out, or telling you in no uncertain terms, 'I want to be alone'. Spend half an hour watching garden birds on a busy feeding station and you'll also see plenty of communication of the 'Push off, this is my peanut' variety.

Talk is cheap

We understand a lot of visual communication because we do it ourselves, with deliberate gestures such as pointing or shrugging the shoulders, and more subconscious ones such as touching our hair. In animals, gestures can evolve into elaborate displays, such as the courtship dances of various birds and fish, which may be emphasised by physical traits such as colourful skin or feathers. Other animal signals are more arcane – for example, the birdsong that epitomises the joy of spring to our ear may in fact signal aggressive territoriality.

Sorry, I didn't catch that

Other forms of animal communication are all but lost on us. We don't hear the rumble of infrasound from elephants or blue whales that carries hundreds of kilometres through ground or water, or the ultrasound twitters of baby mice. We don't generally smell the scented calling cards with

It's real, honest!

Natural selection tends to favour the evolution of **honest signals**. While the tail of a male peacock is clearly blatant advertising, the physiological investment it takes to grow one, keep it in good condition and fly with it means only a high-quality male can pull it off. As such, it is a fairly honest indication of his good breeding.

which most mammals anoint their territories and each other. We don't sense chemical messages or **pheromones** emitted by animals as diverse as horses, fish and beetles, even though air and water may sometimes be thick with them.

Are you impressed yet?

Maybe

Nature's fiercest animals

Nature is often described disparagingly as 'red in tooth and claw', as if it had a choice. For most animals, hunting and self-defence are a matter of survival, but that doesn't mean we can't admire their jaw-dropping strength, skill and ferocity.

For starters, these guys are fairly formidable.

Sperm whale The largest hunter on earth – but it specialises in eating deep-sea squid, which, judging from scars on the head and flank of many whales, often fight back fiercely.

Great white shark Regarded as the terror of the seas, with a torpedo-shaped body up to 6m long and packed with muscle that propels it through the water at up to 40km/h. It locates prey using an electromagnetic sense and an extraordinary sense of smell that will detect one drop of blood in a million drops of water. It attacks with speed and ferocity, applying immense biting force with saw-edged teeth.

Bull shark This species can outbite the great white, but is unable to match the chomping force of **polar bears** or **tigers**.

Saltwater crocodile Has the strongest bite force of any animal.

Did you know?
A group of rhinos is called a crash.

But does killing power equate to ferocity? There is no evidence, for example, that great whites kill for fun or entertainment – something dolphins and domestic cats seem to do routinely.

Both species of African rhinoceros, the black and the white rhino, are known for their bad temper – though the smaller black rhino is more likely to attack and is generally considered more dangerous. A charging rhino can achieve speeds of 60km/h, and weighs 2.5 tonnes.

And the winner is ...

When it comes to sheer hard-as-nails ferocity, the prize goes to a member of the weasel family called the honey badger. This furry power-pack will pick a fight with almost anything. They eat porcupines, shred poisonous snakes and demolish beehives for honey, heedless of venomous bites and stings. They will slaughter baby cheetahs and drive lions from a kill. A honey badger's tough skin is so loose it can turn round to bite an attacker that tries to hang on to almost any part of its body.

Close contenders
- Polar bear
- Leopard seal
- Striated cone snail
- Mantis shrimp
- Black mamba
- Asian giant hornet
- Homo sapiens

Endangered species

Many scientists believe we are living through a mass extinction – the sixth such event to impact life on Earth. The factors contributing to the previous five are somewhat mysterious. But this time the cause is clear. It's us. We are changing the world, and many of our fellow species are losing out.

Extinction has been a fact of life for 3.5 billion years. Of the five billion species of organism estimated to have lived on Earth, 99 per cent are long gone. The process of natural selection, which drives evolution, makes losses inevitable. So, given that we are part of Nature too, why should we worry when species around us dwindle, even if we are the reason? Here are some reasons why.

1 At present, the rate of extinction greatly exceeds that of speciation, or species formation. So biodiversity is declining. Reduced biodiversity leads to fewer checks and balances in natural systems and makes for a clunkier, more volatile system.

2 In our own selfish interest, some of the species being lost might be directly useful to us in ways we don't yet know, such as sources of medicine, or varieties that might transform agriculture or biotechnology.

3 When one species goes extinct, it often carries others with it.

4 Perhaps most powerfully, we are the only species capable of **understanding** extinction, and the only generation capable of saving many species currently teetering on the brink. The losses are happening on our watch, and yet in most cases they are preventable.

Close to home

We are used to the idea of rare and special creatures on the brink of extinction or already gone. For most of us, tigers, orang-utans and northern black rhinos have always been threatened, while dodos, great auks and thylacines have always been extinct. But what if that list includes something very familiar?

A prickly situation

British hedgehogs have been declining at about 5 per cent a year since at least the mid-1990s, when the efforts to monitor them began. In population terms, that is devastatingly fast. The biggest problem hedgehogs face is habitat fragmentation. Hedgehogs can survive in a variety of habitats, including suburban gardens, which can actually be better for them than the wider countryside, but they need to be able to move about to find sufficient food and meet other hedgehogs with which to reproduce. However, they cannot climb, or jump, or even dig very well – so garden fences are insurmountable obstacles. Your garden may be a hedgehog paradise, especially if you avoid using pesticides and leave a few quiet areas for them to forage, but it's no good if they can't get in or out.

All it takes is an opening 13cm square – the size of a CD case – in each boundary. Why not make one today? You can find more details at www.hedgehogstreet.org.

Hedgehogs
THIS WAY

Feathered friends

The 10,000 or so living bird species are all descendants of theropod dinosaurs. Their forelimbs have evolved into wings, they are feathered, reproduce by laying eggs, and share the warm-bloodedness and energetic lifestyle of mammals. Beyond that, their diversity seems to know no limits.

The largest living bird is the ostrich, a flightless African ratite. The smallest bird is the bee hummingbird, weighing as little as 1.6g. One male ostrich weighs as much as 71,500 bee hummingbirds.

The fastest bird – and indeed the fastest self-propelled animal on the planet – is the peregrine falcon. It hunts other birds in flight, cruising above to pick its target then hurling itself vertically downwards at up to 330km/h. This is quite literally breakneck speed – the force of the impact snaps the back or neck of its victim.

Parrots and crows are among the most intelligent animals, with problem-solving intelligence rivalling that of great apes. Many other types of bird have evolved tool use and an ability to pass on knowledge from one generation to the next – known as cultural learning.

Some birds are extremely long-lived – parrots, albatrosses, flamingos and condors all have potential longevity of 80 years, and some captive individuals are claimed to be centenarians. The oldest known wild bird is Wisdom, a female Laysan albatross hatched in 1951 on Midway Atoll and still rearing chicks at the age of 63. Others are certainly much older, but proving the age of untagged wild birds is tricky.

Penguins, auks and ducks are adapted to varying extents for swimming and diving. Their feet are webbed and set far back on the body, reducing their walk to a waddle. In the case of penguins the adaptation is so extreme that flight has had to be sacrificed.

Birds arose in a continuum from non-bird dinosaurs, so it's hard to say exactly when they achieved full bird-hood – like many biological categories, it's an artificial distinction. The honorary title of **First Bird** is traditionally given to *Archaeopteryx lithographica* – a proto-bird that lived in the late Jurassic, 150 million years ago. It had a beak, feathers and wings, though whether these were used for gliding or fully powered flight is unknown.

Flight

Not all birds fly, but those that do achieve it with wings whose cross-sectional shape forms an aerofoil – a slightly humped, tapering profile that forces air to move faster over the top than underneath. This creates a pressure differential above and below the wing – and thus lift.

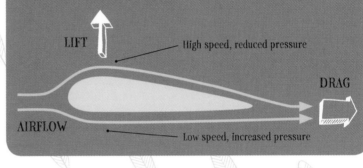

LIFT

High speed, reduced pressure

DRAG

AIRFLOW

Low speed, increased pressure

The most distinctive characteristic of birds is plumage. Feathers are made of keratin, the same protein that grows into hair, horn and claw. Each feather has a central stem, the rachis, bearing barbs, which may be stiff and interlocking, or exceptionally fine and wispy. Some feathers resemble soft fur or shaggy hair, while others appear almost sculptural. Feathers are vital for insulation (possibly their original function), waterproofing, flight and in display.

DIY bird feeder

Feeding wild birds is an easy way to boost the nature value of your garden, yard or windowsill. It may take birds a while to find a new feed station, but persevere and you'll be treated to close views of some of our most engaging wildlife.

You can spend a fortune on feeders, but there's no need. You can make something perfectly adequate using recycled materials, and save your money for the feed!

BIRD FOOD
THIS WAY

You will need
- A 1-litre plastic squash bottle, with lid
- 2 pencils (or use 20cm lengths of slim garden cane)
- Sharp scissors
- Wire to hang

1. Remove the labels, wash out and dry the bottle.

2. Using the scissors, open a pair of feeding ports on opposite sides of the bottle, about 2cm from the bottom. They should be less than 1cm in diameter or they will leak seed.

3. About 1cm below each port, punch a hole just big enough to force the pencils or cane through to form the perches. Repeat for a second pair of ports and perch holes about 10cm up the bottle. Place at right angles to the first pair.

4. Fill the bottle with fat pellets or seed (not peanuts – these should only be fed from mesh feeders that require the birds to break them up in order to remove – whole nuts are a choking hazard). Replace the cap.

5. Use the wire to make a secure loop from which to hang your feeder. Hang from a pole or washing line – ideally in a spot where you can see it but well away from walls, sheds or other structures from which local cats might launch an attack. Bear in mind feeders like this are not squirrel-proof.

Keep it clean

Hygiene is important around garden feeders – busy stations can be a health hazard to birds. Ideally you should wash feeders every couple of weeks in soapy water and dry them thoroughly before refilling. Greenfinches in particular are susceptible to trichomonosis, an easily transmitted and potentially fatal disease. At the first sign of sick-looking birds, withdraw all feeders for two weeks and disinfect thoroughly before reusing (or make new ones).

Best birdie buffet

Aim to supply as many different foods as you can.

Mealworms are ideal for **robins**, **blackbirds** and **wrens**. Live mealworms are more nutritious than dried, but they're expensive and have a habit of metamorphosing into beetles if kept too long.

Stock mixed seeds for **finches**, **tits** and **nuthatches**. It's worth experimenting to find a mix your birds like. Ideally it will contain native seed mixes and little or no wheat. If you don't want weeds around the feeder, look out for 'no-grow' mixes.

Small oily seeds such as niger or thistle are a magnet for **goldfinches**, but require their own feeder with very small feeding apertures.

Fat balls, blocks or pellets are popular with many species, and will probably draw birds to your feed station, especially **tits** and **woodpeckers**, but opinion is divided on the value to birds in terms of breeding success. If you do use them, remove the mesh netting to avoid potentially fatal foot entanglements.

Peanuts are a wonderful winter resource for **tits**, **woodpeckers** and **finches**. Supply them in a mesh feeder or carefully crushed on a table to avoid the risk of choking, and withdraw them from April to July so they are not fed to baby birds. Halved apples will be welcomed in winter.

Insect safari

Insects are the most diverse and abundant group of animals on the planet, with some estimates suggesting that the million species already described are only a tenth of the total. So, not surprisingly, it's usually easy to find a few wherever you live. Let's go insect hunting!

A closer look

The easiest way to capture any very small creepy-crawlies you've trapped is using an inexpensive device called a **pooter**. The pooter has a collecting vessel and two tubes – one with a gauze or mesh, which you put in your mouth, the other which the insect shoots up when you inhale quickly. Make sure you suck the right tube! Then use a hand lens and a field guide to look closely and identify your catch.

Shake sampling

Lay a light-coloured sheet under a tree or shrub and shake the branches vigorously for about 10 seconds. Collect up the edges of the sheet and jiggle the contents towards the middle (otherwise half your catch will escape before you have a chance to see them). Record what you see, even if you can't identify them all, then try a different sort of tree to see how the insect community differs.

Pitfall trap

Dig a hole and sink a flower pot or large yogurt pot with drainage holes punched in the bottom, so that the top is level with the ground. Pack the soil back around it so there are no gaps down the outside, then cover the pot with wire mesh and fix this in place using tent pegs or similar. The mesh squares should be about 1cm to prevent small mammals such as shrews tumbling in – they will die in a matter of hours if trapped. Rig up a rain cover about 5cm above the pitfall using a tile propped up on stones or a square of plastic envelope stiffening material fixed in place with tent pegs. Check the trap morning and evening to see who has stumbled by.

Moth traps

Choose a warm, still, dry night. Hang a white bed sheet from a washing line or a tree at dusk and, as darkness falls, project a bright light, such as a powerful torch or bike lamp, on to it. Then sit by and watch for the night-flying insects that will be attracted. Remember to check both sides of the sheet!

Alternatively, if you actually want to catch the moths, you can use a large plastic garden tub, create a lid from a sheet of white plastic (a large high-quality carrier bag opened out will be fine) and cut a circular opening about 5cm diameter in the middle. Put a bike light at the bottom of the tub, or a string of outdoor LED fairy lights in a loose bundle (not a coil, as this will get hot), along with a few egg boxes to create hiding places for the trapped moths. Turn on the lights, tape the lid firmly in place and leave for a few hours from dusk.

Metamorphosis

Growing up is complicated for most of us – but at least we humans usually end up with the same number of legs and our brain in the same place. Not so for a great many animals, which undergo extraordinary transformations gradually, in a series of step-changes, or in one dramatic reorganisation.

Time for a change

Animals whose development involves **metamorphosis** include jellyfish and corals, molluscs, winged insects, crustaceans, echinoderms (sea urchins and starfish), fish such as lamprey and eels, and amphibians.

The planktonic larvae of various marine invertebrates can differ substantially from the adult forms; the various types of larva have different features and different names, such as pluteus, nauplius, cyprid, zoae, planaria to name just a few.

Just grubbing around

The young stages of winged insects are given a variety of names – grub, maggot, caterpillar, larva, nymph – which mean different things. Grubs, maggots and caterpillars are all **larvae** – but of different types of insect: beetles, flies and lepidopterans (butterflies and moths) respectively. Insects with larvae undergo a dramatic all-in-one **complete metamorphosis**, often while hidden inside an immobile **cocoon**, **chrysalis** or **pupa**. This period is often referred to as a 'resting stage', when in fact it

is anything but restful. Beneath that quiescent exterior, the entire body is being rebuilt out of a soupy chaos of disintegrated self.

Other insects, such as grasshoppers and dragonflies, undergo a series of **partial metamorphosis** events, which take place each time they moult or shed their exoskeleton. These are not larvae but **nymphs**, and each individual's stage or **instar** is a little larger, more complex and adult-looking than the last. The final adult stage of any metamorphosed insect is called an **imago**.

Metamorphosis in fish and amphibians is controlled by two hormones, thyroxin and prolactin. The same two hormones control embryonic development of other vertebrates (including us), though in reptiles, birds and mammals most of the transformation happens inside the egg or the womb.

FROM EGG TO FROG

Frogspawn grow

Tadpole hatches

Hind limbs appear

Forelimbs emerge

Tail shortens

Adult frog – job done!

Frogs and toads develop via an immature stage known as a tadpole. The tadpole is rather fishlike, limbless with external gills. The transition to air-breathing, four-legged adult also includes less obvious changes associated with a switch in feeding ecology from vegetarian grazer to active predator, including the rapid development of large eyes with stereoscopic vision, a muscular tongue and a drastically altered digestive system.

Resilient reptiles

Ask someone to think of a reptile, and they'll probably envisage a snake, a lizard, a crocodile or a dinosaur – possibly a tortoise or turtle. On the face of it this seems to be a fairly clear-cut group. But ask a zoologist and the definition gets a little complicated …

The ancestors of modern birds and mammals were also reptiles, making the traditional classification slightly awkward. In fact historically, reptiles have been variously lumped together with both amphibians and birds. But for practical purposes this class of scaly, cold-blooded creatures makes sense.

I had legs?

Most snakes lay eggs, but some give birth to live young. Unlike amphibians, reptile embryos develop in a watery sac called the amnion, so they are not obliged to breed in water or wet places. All reptiles are classed as tetrapods – or four-legged animals. Tell that to snakes and slowworms! Some legless reptiles such as pythons and boa constrictors still show skeletal evidence of legs, while in others every last vestige of leggedness is gone.

Reptile who's who
There are four main groups of living reptiles.

Squamata, the largest group, includes 9000 species of snake and lizard. They are classified according to the flexible structure of the skull and jaw, which allows them to open their mouths exceptionally wide – large snakes readily ingest prey much larger than themselves. Around 60 per cent of squamates produce venom, including some of the most deadly natural

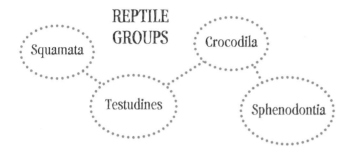

REPTILE GROUPS

- Squamata
- Testudines
- Crocodila
- Sphenodontia

Who'd have thought that we're related?

toxins known. Snakebites kill around 125,000 people every year.

Testudines is a group of 300 different tortoises, turtles and terrapins, distinguished by a hard shell – which forms from extensions of the backbone and ribs. The shell on the back is the carapace; that protecting the underside is the plastron. The group has terrestrial, marine and freshwater members, and the four limbs end in feet or flippers accordingly.

Crocodila or crocodiles are a small group (25 species) of relatively large animals. They are all semi-aquatic, and all are predatory. Several species occasionally attack humans, but not necessarily for food – most incidents occur in the breeding season, when stress levels are naturally high. Most attacks (about 300 a year) are in Africa, by the Nile crocodile.

Sphenodontia has just two species – the New Zealand tuataras. These long-lived reptiles resemble miniature dragons and adopt a slow, low-energy lifestyle that has seen the lineage survive 200 million years, but egg-predation by introduced rats means that they are now highly endangered.

Fish facts

With over 32,000 described species, and plenty more deep-sea types awaiting discovery, fish are by far the world's most diverse group of vertebrate animals, and undisputed masters of the aquatic realm.

Fish are vulnerable to overexploitation. Cod were once considered so abundant off Newfoundland that overfishing seemed impossible. But as fishing methods became more and more efficient and large-scale, by 1992 the Canadian government was obliged to declare a ban on cod fishing in their waters, which is still in place 23 years later.

The deep-sea tripod fish is sometimes called the 'fish with legs'. It doesn't actually have legs, but it can stand, using pectoral and tail fins modified into long spines. It uses this posture to lie in wait for prey.

Sharks are already considered pretty cool by most wildlife enthusiasts. How could you make them cooler? Perhaps discover a new one, a really big one and ... oh, I don't know, make its colossal mouth glow in the dark or something. It sounds like science fantasy, but the megamouth shark, discovered in 1976, is real.

The whale shark is the largest species of fish – with the biggest specimens exceeding 12m in length and weighing over 20 tonnes. Like many very large marine creatures, it is a filter feeder, eating mainly plankton and shoals of small fish.

The oarfish, the world's longest bony fish at up to 11m, is probably the origin of sea serpent myths. With its large eyes, silvery body and red crest, it's certainly dramatic-looking, but is rarely seen alive.

Central heating for fish

Everyone knows fish are cold-blooded. Except some aren't. Several species of shark, tuna and billfish can warm parts of their body, particularly the brain and eyes, using muscle heat. And at least one species, the opah, uses a heat-exchange system in its gills to conserve warmth so that the whole body is warmed to about five degrees above ambient temperature.

There are three contenders for the fastest fish in the ocean – the sailfish, swordfish and striped marlin. All are billfish, torpedo-like predators boasting bodies packed with muscle. Speeds in excess of 100km/h are reported for all three.

Male and female anglerfish are so different they were originally classified as separate species. The male is tiny and, having found a female in the darkness of the deep sea, he clamps on with his mouth and their flesh and blood supplies fuse – he becomes a wholly dependent parasite, available 24/7 to fertilise her eggs when the time comes to spawn.

The famous zoologist Niko Tinbergen revealed the humble three-spined stickleback to have a complex courtship and breeding biology. Male sticklebacks build nests and perform ritual dances to attract females to spawn, then care devotedly for the eggs and fry. Breeding males flush red and react violently to the colour – Tinbergen's specimens lived in a tank near a window and went into a frenzy when the post van passed by each day.

Micro-life

The idea of life forms too small to see with the naked eye was proposed by early scientific thinkers in India, ancient Rome and the Muslim world more than 2,000 years ago. But proof required optical technology that didn't arrive until the 17th century.

Life through a lens

The science of **microbiology** owes its beginning to a Dutchman, Antonie van Leeuwenhoek, who worked as a draper in the 1650s. Unsatisfied with the quality of magnifying glasses available for seeing the quality of thread in the cloth he bought and sold, he began grinding his own lenses, and around 1676 developed an entirely new method using minute

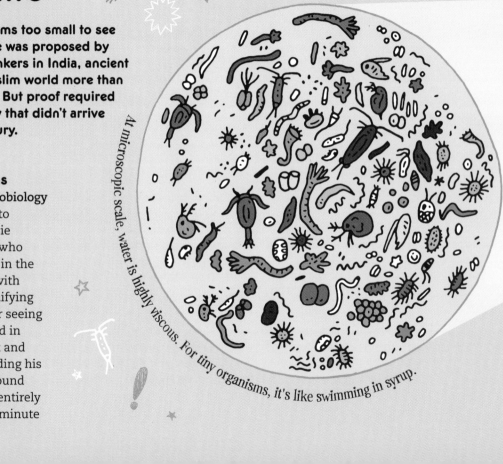

At microscopic scale, water is highly viscous. For tiny organisms, it's like swimming in syrup.

A micro-organism is too small to be seen by the naked eye.

The best early microscopes achieved magnification of 500x.

Micro-organisms exceed macroscopic (visible) life in terms of biomass.

spheres of glass. These tiny blobs provided much greater magnification but were fiddly to use, so van Leeuwenhoek created a small device in which the lens and the sample could be mounted and adjusted to best effect. This was the first microscope, and with it van Leeuwenhoek entered a new world.

A clear view

In the space of a few years he became the first person to see single-celled organisms such as **protists** and **bacteria** (which he called 'animalcules'), and also the first to describe sperm, the detailed anatomy of various small animals such as insects, and the fine structure of tissues such as muscle.

Further developments that depended on the microscope include the discovery and description of the **cell** by Robert Hooke and the development of germ theory by Louis Pasteur and Robert Koch, who showed the link between certain micro-organisms and disease.

Now you see it ...

Micro-organisms are classified in a variety of major groups, including viruses, bacteria, protozoans, algae, micro-animals and Archaea. The archaeans are single-celled organisms that thrive virtually everywhere on Earth, including extreme environments such as boiling-hot springs. Examples of many of these types can often be found in a single drop of pond water.

Glossary

Antioxidant A chemical the limits oxidation, a chemical reaction which produces volatile and potentially damaging molecules (free radicals)

Aquifer A natural underground reservoir of water stored in permeable rock, sand or gravel

Archipelago A group of islands

Biodiversity The variety of different forms of life (usually species, subspecies or genetic variants)

Carbon footprint An estimate of the total greenhouse gas (carbon dioxide) emissions produced by a person, group or activity

Cell Basic functional unit of living things

Climate (climatology) The long-term pattern of weather (and study of)

Community (biological) A group of species share a habitat and interact with one another

Crustacean Members of the Class Crustacea, including crabs, shrimps, lobsters, barnacles, copepods and lice

Deciduous Trees that shed their leaves in winter

Dicotyledons Flowering plants whose seedlings develop with two embryonic seed leaves (cotyledons)

Electromagnetic radiation Energy emitted from sources such as our Sun, having wavelike and particle like properties. Examples include gamma rays, x-rays, ultraviolet, visible light, infrared, microwaves and radio waves

Epidemic The rapid spread of an infectious disease within a population

Erosion The removal of soil or rock, for example by the action of water, wind, ice or interference such as digging and footfall.

Evaporation Transition of a liquid to a gaseous state

Fossil The preserved remains of a long-dead organism

Gene The unit of inheritance, physically a length of deoxyribonucleic acid (DNA) on a chromosome

Genetic bottleneck A sudden sharp reduction in the size of a population, leading to smaller genetic variability in later generations

Geology The study of rocks

Germination The process by which a new plant begins to grow from a seed

Hemisphere Half of the globe, usually as divided north/south by the Equator

Heritable (in terms of genetics) Capable of being passed on from one generation to the next

Hormone A biological molecule used in signalling within a single organism

Invertebrate An animal without a backbone

Lava Rock ejected onto the Earth's surface in a molten state

Logarithmic scale Non-linear scale in which each increment represents an order of magnitude

Magma Molten rock beneath the Earth's surface

Meteorite A piece of space debris that has fallen to Earth

Meterology Study of weather

Molecule Smallest unit of a chemical compound or element, made up of two or more atoms

Mollusc A member of the phylum Mollusca, including snails, clams, slugs and octopi

Monocotyledons Flowering plants whose seedlings develop with one embryonic seed leaf (cotyledon), grasses lilies and palms

Nivial Referring to snow

Organic (chemistry) Containing carbon

Organism A living thing

Parasite An organism that lives at the expense of another – often on or inside the host

Pesticide A poison used for killing unwelcome animals

Pigment A naturally occurring compound that gives plants and animals colour

Plankton Communities of small, generally microscopic water life

Polychaete One of three main groups of segmented worm or Annelid, including the ragworms and tubeworms. Other annelids include earthworms and leeches

Prosthetic A replacement body part

Protein Organic, nitrogen-containing compounds made up of chains of amino acids, produced by all living things and forming a major part of biological structures

Protist A catchall term for a variety of microscopic, mainly single-celled organisms, now assigned to a variety of biological classifications including amoebas, dinoflagellates, foraminiferans and red algae

Refraction The bending of light as it passed through mediums of different density, such as air and water

Seismic (seismo-) Concerning earthquakes or vibrations in the Earth's crust

Solar Referring to the Sun

Stamen Male (pollen-producing) reproductive part of a flower

Stigma Part of a flower where pollen is received

Sublimation Transition from solid to gas without passing through a liquid phase

Tannin Bitter-tasting compounds (polyphenols) often produced by plants to deter herbivores

Terrestrial Of the Earth/land-dwelling

Theropoda A diverse group of dinosaurs, some which were the direct ancestors of birds

Topography The shape of surfaces – for example of planets and landmasses (and the study thereof)

Tsunami Wave or surge of displaced water, usually in a ocean, generated by an earthquake, volcanic eruption or other large disturbance

Venomous Capable of producing and injecting toxin (venom), usually by means of a bite or sting

Wavelength (of electromagnetic radiation) The distance between consecutive peaks in an electromagnetic wave. In the visible spectrum, red light has a longer wavelength than violet. Gamma and X rays have short wavelengths, radio and microwaves have long wavelengths

'Come forth into the light of things, let nature be your teacher.'

William Wordsworth

Thanks William, we will. Meanwhile, did you know... WOMBAT POOP IS CUBIC?!? #CoolNature